"I am prepared to stake my evening's winnings. What can you offer me in return?"

Dominic looked round wildly. Here was a chance to recoup all he had lost and more if he could put up something that might be equal in value to the thousands of guineas and vowels under Hawkeworth's fingers. In a sudden moment of desperate clarity, he knew he should never have gambled at all, particularly in view of their gloomy future. Sarah would never forgive him. Then it came to him in a flash. Sarah. He would have a stake just as good as this Marquess's with her.

Hawkeworth sat drumming his fingers idly on the table and waiting for his response, while Henderson's snores echoed gently round them.

"I will stake my sister," Dominic said, his voice sounding loud in his own ears. "My sister against your winnings."

DEBT
OF
HONOUR

Elizabeth Carey

FAWCETT COVENTRY • NEW YORK

Chapter 1

The candles flickered as the door opened and then closed again behind the figure of a young lady. She paused for an instant on the threshold, surveying the room, then moved quickly across to the large curtained bed in one corner.

"How do you feel now, Nanny?" she murmured. "I have ordered a glass of milk to be sent up to you here, and knowing how much faith you had in such a remedy for us as children, I know you will feel better after drinking it. Anyway, I mean to stay here until you do," she added firmly, as she sat down on a low chair by the bed.

"Sarah, what would I do without you?" the old woman murmured weakly. She reached out and grasped the hand of the girl in her own. "I wish that I felt stronger, for I should be waiting upon you and seeing you comfortably bestowed in this place and not the other way around." The old voice grew firmer. "We should never have stopped here in this low tavern, you know, dear. There are many more exclusive hotels which would have been far more suitable. Your mother would never have countenanced this inn, of that I'm certain."

Reassured by the gentle grumbling, Sarah settled

down in her chair, but her smile betrayed her own uneasiness. However, she strove to hide her anxiety and to soothe her companion. "You mustn't fret so, Nanny dear, or you will wear yourself out, and you must be fit in the morning or your sister will wonder what we have done to you."

"Mary will be that pleased to see me again she will never stop talking long enough to bother with my appearance," Nanny returned tartly. "But this inn is not a fit place for a young girl like you. It seems to be more like a gentlemen's club than a hotel for respectable folk."

"Dominic learned of the Thatched House Tavern from friends before we left Sussex," Sarah said quietly. "It is famous for serving excellent meals, and you must admit the dinner we shared earlier was very good."

"That's as may be," Nanny sniffed. "We were still the only females dining downstairs, and that was enough for me. Your brother should have bespoken rooms at Grenier's or even the Star."

Privately Sarah agreed with her old nurse. She had felt slightly uneasy as soon as the carriage that had brought them to London stopped outside the inn at the bottom of St. James's Street that afternoon. Her fears had grown when she noticed how the men passing by stared at her and when she saw no other ladies in the public rooms of the hotel. She had been grateful to Dominic for securing three chambers for them quickly so that she could escape the curious stares, but she had again been subjected to close scrutiny throughout dinner and had found herself growing too uncomfortable to enjoy the excellent array of dishes placed before them. Dominic had no such scruples and, as soon as he decently could, had left his sister and his old nurse to retire abovestairs and had joined an acquaintance he had met earlier in the bar. It transpired he had soon found other friends, or so he told his sister before going out.

"I was up at Oxford with Jamie St. Clair. He's a grand chap, and so is his friend George Henderson. I'm joining them both to share a glass or two and to see some of the sights this evening," he admitted when Sarah questioned him. "You don't mind if I leave you? I will stay if you want me to," he added with a martyred sigh.

"No. You must go and enjoy yourself," Sarah insisted at once. "I am tired, and when I have seen Nanny comfortably settled I will go to bed. But don't forget we have to present ourselves to Lady Marchmont tomorrow."

"I won't forget, sis. Stop worrying." Anxious to be off, Dominic had only paused long enough to settle his wig in front of the mirror and adjust his satin coattails before disappearing. That had been several hours ago, and Sarah was already growing a little worried that he might not return before dawn.

As if reading her thoughts, Nanny sniffed again. "That brother of yours should have been here to take care of you. Any of the fine gentlemen we saw below could make off with you and he be none the wiser. It's his responsibility now your father's dead and buried. God rest his soul," she murmured respectfully. "Young Dominic is head of the house now and must see to your future."

Sarah laughed, and her worry lessened slightly. "I cannot see Dominic as the head of the family somehow, Nanny, and I hope Lady Marchmont will be able to help with my future. She is my mother's aunt, after all, and our only living relative."

"Except for that pompous stepbrother of yours who inherited the estate, damn him!" Nanny muttered with unwonted ferocity. The strain of losing her temper even briefly made her gasp, and she lay back on her pillows wearily. Her wrinkled face was lined and anxious under the frilly nightcap, and Sarah patted her hand reassuringly.

7

"Don't fret so. It is hardly the fault of poor Thomas that my father was unable to provide for us, the children of his second marriage. Thomas will make a success of running the estate, I'm sure, in a way that poor Papa never could."

"Your father was only interested in his old books and papers!"

"He was a scholar," Sarah reproved the old servant gently. "Since he was a second son himself he never expected to be the squire and had no taste for estate management when he suddenly came into the inheritance. I do hope that Lady Marchmont will remember us all, though. She never answered either of my letters."

"You should have accepted your half brother's hospitality until you did hear," Nanny argued at once. "It was foolish to come all the way up to London without an invitation."

"I wanted to see you settled with your sister," Sarah replied as cheerfully as she could. She was grateful for the tap on the door that heralded the arrival of the hot milk. She had no wish to defend Dominic yet again from Nanny's criticisms, which she knew were justified. Her brother was impetuous and hotheaded, always rushing into things without considering the consequences. He disliked his half brother and had no wish to accept grudging hospitality, particularly as Thomas had a large brood of unruly children, and Sarah had agreed with him. But as she accepted the tray from the servant who stood outside she sighed to herself. If Lady Marchmont was unwilling to recognize the relationship or unable to assist them, then their future would be precarious.

Nanny, who had nursed Sarah through all the childish ailments and loved her in place of the mother who had died at her birth, guessed some of the thoughts passing through the girl's head. As she looked at the slim, upright figure bearing the tray across the room the old woman sighed too. Sarah was lovely but too willful to be let loose alone in London; she needed strong protection, which was now denied her after the death of her father three months before. Dominic was a good boy, but wild, and Nanny wished her charges had someone they could turn to.

She watched the girl lovingly and thought again that few young ladies were as charming as her nursling. Sarah had light-brown hair which curled into fashionable ringlets and framed her face delicately, giving her an ethereal look which was deceptive. Her eyes were green and could sparkle with rage when she was thwarted but were now filled with loving affection as she proffered the soothing drink to her nurse. The girl herself knew that her dainty figure and fragile appearance could influence even strong men, and she had often avoided just punishment by her wistful appeals to her father and brothers. Yet this same charm could be her downfall if Lady Marchmont took a dislike to her. Nanny sipped the milk and wondered what the future held.

"You will come to me if you need me, won't you?" she asked sleepily. "There is not much room in Mary's house, but we can all fit in, I'm sure. Promise me."

"Of course I will come to see you in your little cottage," Sarah promised at once. "Although I doubt if you will really enjoy retirement, Nanny. I hope that when Lady Marchmont has arranged a splendid marriage for me you will come back and take charge of my children and look after them the same way you did us."

The old woman smiled at this and nodded, but the milk had served its purpose and in no time she had drifted off to sleep. Relieved, Sarah got up from the bedside and quietly left the room to cross the corridor into her own chamber. Her maid, Annie, was sitting dozing by the fire. She sat up quickly, startled by the sudden appearance of her mistress.

"Oh, Miss Sarah, you did give me a fright. How is Mrs. Pemberton now? Is she sleeping? You should have let me sit with her. It's not right for you to be attending to her, that it isn't." Annie bustled around laying out a nightrobe as she spoke.

"Nonsense, Annie. Nanny would never have settled down if I had not been with her," Sarah replied absently. "Have you heard from Edward if Master Dominic has returned yet?"

This reference to Edward, the master's valet, made Annie blush scarlet. Hiding her embarrassment, she began to undo the fastenings of her mistress's blue silk gown and mumbled a reply. "I did see him a while back. Master Dominic told him not to wait up as he expected to be late."

"Oh dear!" Sarah exclaimed without thinking. She stood in the middle of the room clad only in her petticoats and wide hoop. "I do hope he will not do anything foolish, particularly as we must see Lady Marchmont as soon as possible tomorrow."

Annie, a plump and homely girl only a few years older than her mistress, knew all about the problems besetting the Davenant family. She had discussed the matter with her intended, Edward, the master's valet, on many occasions of late, for their own future was closely involved.

"I'm sure he will remember such an important meeting, and he will feel tired after the journey up from the country." Annie was practical, and because she herself was weary from traveling she expected her employers to feel the same way.

Relieved of her cumbersome hoop by Annie's deft fingers, Sarah was not so certain of her brother's sense of responsibility. He had been so excited at the prospect of this trip to London and had seized on the excuse offered by the need to meet Lady Marchmont as much as his dislike of accepting his stepbrother's charity to hasten their departure. He had been full of energy and enthusiasm when he bade her farewell earlier in the evening, and Sarah could only hope he did not fall into bad company so soon after his arrival.

Her worst fears were not realized, and on waking next morning Sarah was pleased to hear from Annie that Dominic had reached the Thatched House Tavern at a respectable hour and was even now breaking his fast and would join her as soon as he had dressed. This took longer than Sarah had anticipated, since Dominic intended to create a good impression on his unknown relative and consequently changed his mind and his coat four times in half an hour and took twice that long to tie his cravat.

She had to admit he looked splendid when he did appear and as handsome as any of the gallants she had yet seen parading up and down St. James's Street. His fair hair was closely cropped and hidden under a neat brown wig that gave him an air of sober respectability, which was belied by the twinkle in his blue eyes and the dashing cut of his crimson twilled silk coat with black froggings and silver buttons. His nether garments were palest beige, and the black shoes sported buckles of silver to match his coat, while his linen did great credit to Edward's attentions.

"My! You look very impressive!" Sarah exclaimed. "Where did you get those clothes? I have never seen that coat before. Surely you have not had time to shop yet, Dom?"

Her brother looked a trifle sheepish and shook his head. "I ordered 'em before we left Lewes. Thought I ought to have a new coat and all that to meet Lady Marchmont. Must create a good impression at the beginning, Sarah," he insisted hopefully.

"I know we must, but if she should refuse to help us, where will we get the money to pay for such finery?" she objected.

He shrugged his shoulders impatiently. "It's not as bad as that yet, Sarah. I know Father left us almost nothing, but I can still pay the shot. Anyway, the fellows I met last night promised to take me to a club where I can be sure of making the most of what I've got and more," he boasted.

"Not by gambling, Dom. Oh, no!" she said in horror. "You can never make money that way but only lose what little you do have."

"I never said anything about gambling, did I?" he snapped back irritably. "Don't be silly, Sarah, and don't jump to conclusions like that. Now let's be off. Edward has brought the carriage around from the stables. So are you ready to go?"

"Yes indeed. I feel rather nervous, though, don't you, Dom? What if she takes a dislike to us?" Sarah whispered apprehensively.

He squeezed her arm reassuringly. "Course she'll like us. Can't fail to. Don't worry, sis."

Cheered by his confidence and Nanny's good wishes, Sarah managed to ignore the stares of the curious as she left the tavern and climbed into the carriage with Annie beside her. Dominic followed and gave the address in Hanover Square that his father had pressed upon him in his last moments. As they bowled along he chatted happily about the people he had met the previous evening and described the passing sights in his usual carefree manner.

By the time they reached the front of the imposing residence in Hanover Square, Sarah was almost as cheerful as her brother and already beginning to plan how soon they could move into her aunt's house from the Thatched House Tavern.

Dominic helped his sister alight from the carriage and led her up the steps to the front door. "You did say we would call today?" he inquired with the first sign of hesitation he had shown. "Don't look very welcoming."

"You can hardly expect her to meet us on the doorstep," Sarah whispered back. "After all, we have only met once and she may take a while to grow accustomed to us."

"Or we to her, more likely," he muttered as he rapped on the knocker.

The footman who opened the door regarded them distantly and asked their business. Somewhat annoyed, Dominic said haughtily: "We have come to see Lady Marchmont. Mr. Dominic Davenant and Miss Sarah Davenant."

The footman's expression changed. He looked warily at them. "Lord Marchmont is not at home," he replied carefully.

"We have come to see Lady Marchmont," Dominic repeated as if to an idiot. "Pray announce us at once."

The footman gazed at them uncertainly. "Lord Marchmont is unmarried," he intoned as if this settled the matter.

"We have come to see Lady Marchmont," Sarah intervened, unable to keep quiet any longer.

"Ah! Lady Marchmont. Ah yes." Understanding dawned on the man's face, but to their surprise he closed the door on them without another word.

Dominic stared at Sarah in amazement which quickly changed to fury. He raised his hand to strike the door knocker another blow, but before his hand could move the door opened again and a very superior personage confronted them. "If you would be so good as to step inside," this worthy murmured.

He ushered them into a huge hall tiled in marble with a wide sweeping staircase rising up from one side lined with marble busts. They were shown into a small withdrawing room on the ground floor before another word was spoken.

"I am Ponsonby, Lord Marchmont's butler. May I tell him you called?" the portly servant murmured deferentially.

Dominic was fast losing patience, but before he could explode, Sarah repeated what she had said to the footman. "We wish to speak to Lady Marchmont. She is

13

our great-aunt, and I have written to her. We are expected."

Ponsonby shook his head sadly. "I am afraid not, Miss Davenant," he replied. "Lady Marchmont died not two months ago. Lord Marchmont—a distant relative, you understand—has only recently arrived in London. Do you wish me to tell him you called?"

"Died?" Dominic repeated in stunned tones. "Died, you say?"

"Yes sir. I regret to say so. I believe Lady Marchmont was much loved."

"And a relative has inherited her estate?" Sarah put in quickly.

"That is correct. A distant relation is the present Lord Marchmont. Now . . ." He coughed discreetly. "His lordship should be returning later today. Will you wait?"

"No. No. We will call another day," Sarah said hurriedly. "Come, Dominic." She took hold of his arm, and he allowed her to lead him out of the house and said nothing until the carriage was once more on the move.

"With Lady Marchmont dead, what can we do now?" he exclaimed as they drove down St. James's Street. "Where can we go?"

Chapter 2

Dominic's depression did not last long. By the evening his natural optimism had reasserted itself, and he joined his newfound friends full of confidence. Sarah was left feeling thoroughly miserable with a long evening to endure in her room with only her maid for company, as Nanny had already gone to her house.

His sister's loneliness did not deter Dominic from his plans; as he confided to Jamie St. Clair, "When I return full of juice in the morning she will be delighted."

"I can promise you excellent company and the chance of a fine game or two at the Cocoa Tree," Jamie responded cheerfully. "Don't you agree, George? We will show him how to live this evening."

"Oh, certainly. You can rely on us both, Dominic. Jamie here is up to all the rigs in town, and what he doesn't know is not worth bothering about." George grinned and slapped his friend on the back happily. He was a pleasant but vacuous young man of ample fortune and little brain who relied on his associates to help him out of the scrapes he invariably fell into. "We can even have some sport with the Watch later or try the Roundhouse for the night," he added enthusiastically.

Dominic hastily demurred. "Oh, I think I would

prefer to keep to the tables tonight and try my luck there first. I doubt if Sarah would approve of bailing me out tomorrow."

"I doubt if she would," Jamie agreed solemnly. "But you know, Dom, you must forget that sister of yours for the night. Devilish pretty and all that, but women can spoil a man's enjoyment of life, d'ye know? I have the same problem, only mine's with my mother. Just come with us to the Cocoa Tree and enjoy yourself."

"Will there be any difficulty about my getting in?" Dominic inquired later as they walked along St. James's Street in the direction of the club.

"None at all," Jamie assured him. "I'm well known there, and so is George. The stakes are high enough, but not so steep as at White's, nor is the place so exclusive. Couldn't get you into White's, but you'll enjoy the Cocoa Tree better, I'm sure. Fewer stuffy old men around to complain about us youngsters." He laughed. "We can always go to Arthur's if we find the company thin here," he added. He turned into the portals of the Cocoa Tree, once a chocolate house and now a gaming club for the rich aristocracy.

The evening began well for Dominic. He stayed at the hazard tables and the dice fell for him so that his meager store of gold soon multiplied enormously, giving him a sense of elation.

"We must celebrate your success with a bottle or two before settling down to serious gambling," Jamie suggested boisterously. "What do you say?"

His companions readily agreed, and wine flowed freely among them. Dominic, normally an abstemious young man not given to drinking more than a glass or two, soon found himself pleasantly excited with a heady feeling that his luck was in. "Let's join a pharaoh table now. I believe the cards will go my way tonight,"

"Shall we join Marchmont's table?" Jamie asked George Henderson thoughtfully. "I see Hawkeworth is there too, and Trevenning."

16

Before Henderson could reply, Dominic broke into the conversation, suddenly sobered by the mention of that name. "Marchmont?" he asked quickly. "Did you say Lord Marchmont is here?"

"I did. Over there standing beside Sir Peter Trevenning and the Marquess of Hawkeworth. Do you know him?"

"No. But a great-aunt of ours was related to him, so I've heard. He might even be connected, I suppose," Dominic said slowly. "Can we join that table?"

"No reason why not," Jamie said cheerfully. "Is there, George? I'm surprised to see Marchmont and Hawkeworth playing at the same table, though. Thought they were rivals for the affections of the fair Delia."

"They are," George agreed. "Maybe they are deciding who shall have her over a throw of the cards."

His frivolous suggestion was taken seriously by St. Clair. "Would be playing piquet if that was the idea," he corrected. "Can't decide such a thing over the pharaoh table."

"No. You're right, Jamie. Still, I wonder which man will win her affections. I even thought of trying myself," he added. "Do you think I would stand a chance with the toast of London society?" he asked wistfully.

"Definitely not, George," Jamie said, but not unkindly. "You might be plump in the pocket, but you're not rich enough for Delia Masterson. Her mama intends her to marry one of the biggest fortunes in town, and one with a title if possible."

"I was afraid of that. Well, I suppose Hawkeworth will get her then. Seems a shame."

Dominic was growing bored with the conversation, which held no interest for him. He had been studying Lord Marchmont and was disappointed in what he saw. The man was of medium height but his face was thin and sharp-featured and his expression sour at this moment. His clothes were elegant, but the height of his wig emphasized his foppish inclinations, and Dominic

17

noted with disgust that he wore red high-heeled shoes and sported patches and face paint. His first view of the man did not inspire in him any hope that Marchmont might help them in his dead great-aunt's place, and his instinctive dislike led him to make one of his first mistakes of the evening.

He turned to his friends with some idea of perhaps trying to win aid from this man rather than ask for it. "Why don't we stop talking and begin playing?" he said eagerly. "Let us join the table at once."

"Stakes could be quite high," Jamie demurred, suddenly remembering Dominic was not nearly so well off as he and Henderson were. "Could find another table with lower stakes, y'know."

"No. I want to play at that one with Lord Marchmont," Dominic said with drunken determination.

Jamie shrugged and walked across. He made suitable introductions, and apart from a few raised eyebrows Dominic was accepted by the company on his recommendation. However, as the young man watched the cards taken one by one from the box, he heard Marchmont hiss loudly: "Seems we must put up with riffraff from the country now. Tiresome bore."

Trevenning, who was a kindly man, noted the angry flush on the young man's cheeks, proving he had heard the malicious remark. He said pleasantly, "It is a welcome change to have fresh faces at the tables." He smiled at Dominic as he said this.

Beside him Hawkeworth drawled softly, "And fresh fortunes, eh?"

Trevenning shook his head. "I doubt if he has well-lined pockets, somehow," he murmured, too quietly to be heard by other people gathered around the table. "St. Clair should have introduced him to another table where the stakes are lower."

"Quite right. Well, I for one have no wish to milk the pigeon. It is too easy and therefore deadly boring."

Hawkeworth raised one hand to his mouth to stifle a yawn, and Trevenning laughed.

"You know you don't really mean that, Gerry. Why do you come here otherwise?"

"To enjoy your scintillating company, Peter, of course," Hawkeworth replied and raked in his winnings with a languid hand.

"More likely just to annoy dear Marchmont by winning when he is banker," Trevenning muttered.

Gerald, Marquess of Hawkeworth, grinned wickedly, and his black eyebrows rose a fraction. He turned his attention back to the game and watched the newcomers to the table begin to lose their money almost as fast as he was winning it. He knew that both Henderson and St. Clair had comfortable fortunes, but from the hectic flush on the face of the other young man, Davenant, he could ill afford to gamble as recklessly as he seemed intent on doing. One by one many of the older members of the club drifted away from the table, and soon only Hawkeworth, Trevenning, Marchmont, and the three young men remained.

Already Hawkeworth, who now held the bank, had been forced to accept vowels from Davenant, as he had already done from his two companions, but he doubted if the young man had the means to settle his account. At first he had viewed his rashness with amusement, seeing in the frowning brow and scowling glances shot at Marchmont another man who disliked the new peer. But now that the bank had changed hands he sensed only desperation to recoup earlier losses, and for a fleeting moment he was sorry for this young fellow, a rare emotion for him.

Dominic was regretting the bottles of wine they had drunk so fast before the game began. He had only the haziest idea of what he had lost, but it seemed that his early good fortune had quite deserted him. He had been unable to win anything substantial from Marchmont, to his disgust, and now he seemed to be losing a great deal to the black-browed, haughty gentleman who had taken his place.

"I think it's about time the bank closed for the night," Hawkeworth murmured and stood up wearily. He hoped by so doing he could prevent the young fool from losing more, and he saw the momentary expression of relief that flitted across Davenant's face.

"Afraid Miss Masterson will learn you have been winning from babes now, are you?" Marchmont put in with false sweetness. "Are you planning to change your image for her, Hawkeworth?"

The marquess paused with one hand still on the box of cards. His nostrils flared and his lips thinned angrily, and he flicked off Trevenning's restraining arm. "I hope you will rephrase that, Marchmont, or be prepared to back your words with action," he snapped.

Before Marchmont could reply, Dominic, realizing he had been slighted, thrust himself forward. "If you are referring to me as a babe, my lord, I object. I have every wish to go on playing, if Lord Hawkeworth will continue."

Marchmont smiled to himself at the success of his intervention. He threw in his own hand and watched with interest as a furious Hawkeworth sat down again and prepared for another round. He would have preferred to issue a challenge to Marchmont, but it had not needed Trevenning's warning pressure on his arm to dissuade him from such a course. The man was trying to provoke him, hoping that he would do something outrageous that would remove him as a suitor in the running for Miss Masterson's hand. Although he was sorry for young Davenant and had no idea why Marchmont had picked on this young man to vent his spite, Hawkeworth refused either to bow to the insult or demand satisfaction, and he was irritated to discover that Marchmont seemed very pleased by the developments so far.

St. Clair dropped out of the game with muttered

excuses and Henderson was too drunk and sleepy to continue successfully, but both men sensed the atmosphere around the table although they were unaware of the cause and stayed propped up beside Davenant to give him some support by their presence.

The cards continued to fall badly for Dominic, and his desperation increased. Sweat was pouring down his face and he wanted to tear off his wig, for the heat seemed to be stifling him. Again and again it seemed to him he lost his money, and the frown on the banker's face was such that he quaked at the thought of meeting him later and admitting he could not pay his debts. And still the odious Marchmont stood beside the table watching his every move with apparent delight.

When he was about to give in and admit the disaster that lay in front of him, Dominic found that Hawkeworth was suddenly smiling at him.

"Since we are now the only two remaining and I am bored in my position as banker, I want to propose one last throw of the cards, ace high. I am prepared to stake my evening's winnings. What can you offer me in return?"

Dominic looked around wildly. Here was a chance to recoup all he had lost and more if he could put up something that might be equal in value to the thousands of guineas and vowels under Hawkeworth's fingers. In a sudden moment of desperate clarity he knew he should never have gambled at all, particularly in view of their gloomy future. Sarah would never forgive him. Then it came to him in a flash. Sarah. He would have a stake just as good as this marquess's with her.

Hawkeworth sat drumming his fingers idly on the table and waiting for his response while Henderson's snores echoed gently around them.

"I will stake my sister," Dominic said, his voice sounding loud in his own ears. "My sister against your winnings." He stared defiantly across the table, glad that at this moment the odious Marchmont had been called away by an acquaintance and only Trevenning was witness to his proposition.

The marquess paused, and his brows drew together. "You cannot accept such a bet," whispered Sir Peter in a scandalized tone. "Think what people will say!"

"No one need know, Peter," Hawkeworth replied, a gleam of mischief lighting up his eyes and making his face seem younger and more attractive. "That is, unless you tell them. It will do him no harm to have such a fright, and he will be no worse off tomorrow, whatever the outcome, I assure you."

Trevenning gasped his relief and relaxed. He himself shuffled the cards and dealt one to each of the men while St. Clair's snores mingled with those of Henderson and the gentle hum of conversation from other parts of the room.

Dominic, white-faced and trembling, flipped over his card, unaware of how unorthodox the whole proceedings had become, only knowing that he must win whatever happened. His card was the five of spades, and as he watched, Hawkeworth turned over the queen of hearts. He had lost. Sarah, his own sister, was now the property of this man opposite.

"Best of three," Hawkeworth said swiftly and nudged Trevenning to pick up the cards before the younger man recovered his wits. Trevenning did so and shuffled again. As if in a dream, Dominic turned over the second card to see a knave of diamonds, and his hopes rose only to be dashed when Hawkeworth turned up the ace of clubs.

He rose stiffly to his feet and bowed awkwardly. "If you will meet me at the Thatched House Tavern in the morning, gentlemen, I will settle my debts," he murmured, unable to say more.

St. Clair stumbled to his feet at Dominic's nudge and Henderson was rudely shaken awake by Trevenning while Hawkeworth ignored all of them and calmly collected the guineas and notes of hand that had been lying in front of him.

At that moment Lord Marchmont returned, and his keen glance took in the group and noticed Trevenning's dismay, Hawkeworth's calm indifference, and Davenant's shocked horror. "The game has finished, gentlemen?" he asked, ignoring Davenant's drunken companions completely.

"It has," Trevenning said abruptly. "We bid you goodnight." He turned his back to talk to the marquess.

Marchmont ignored this slight and remained beside Davenant. "You lost?" he inquired with apparent concern. "Not too much, I hope, on your first night here."

"No, no. It's not the money," Dominic muttered wretchedly. "But my sister."

"Your sister?" Marchmont murmured. "She will be annoyed with you, I suppose. It is always thus with one's female relatives."

"I don't mean that. I lost her. I used my sister as a stake and lost."

His wretchedness was so great he could hardly contain himself, and for once Marchmont was speechless. But as he shepherded the trio out of the Cocoa Tree and along St. James's Street his mind was racing with this tidbit, and he had obtained the full details of the evening's events before he left the unfortunate Dominic on the doorstep of the Thatched House Tavern.

The Marquess of Hawkeworth had seen Marchmont latch on to the young men, and his expression grew grim. "I hope that young pup can keep a still tongue," he murmured.

"And if he does not?" Trevenning said in ill-disguised dismay.

"Then I have won myself a woman," Hawkeworth drawled and moved off before Trevenning could say more.

Chapter 3

Sarah woke next morning with a feeling of lethargy, and even as she sipped her chocolate she knew the reason was that she had nothing to look forward to. She had wanted to come up to London almost as much as Dominic had, and for both of them it was their first real opportunity to sample the life of the capital. Their father had preferred the quiet retired life he led on his estates and had seen no reason to change it or bother with the round of fashionable life; and as her mother had died at her birth, Sarah had no one to introduce her into society. She had pinned her hopes on Lady Marchmont's sponsoring her instead. Now she knew this was an impossible dream and that within the next few days they must leave and return to Sussex to become unwanted guests living on the grudging hospitality of their half brother. In her case, she decided, she would have to find some kind of gainful employment.

She sighed heavily, and Annie stopped bustling around laying out her clothes and looked at her in sympathy. "It do seem a shame, Miss Sarah, that the old lady has died before you got a chance to see her. Did you think of meeting Lord Marchmont and asking him for help instead?"

This thought had just been going through Sarah's own mind, but she had no wish for Annie to guess that. "There is a chance he might do something for us," she said, as if the idea had only just occurred to her. "But if he is some sort of cousin of the late Lady Marchmont he might not even be related to us at all and probably has no wish to be saddled with stray members of the family."

"He must be related to you if he was cousin to Lady Marchmont, surely," Annie insisted. "She was your mother's aunt, so you told me."

"Yes, she was," Sarah agreed. "Father told us to go to her when he was dying, for he had no relations of his own living at all. Oh dear! It's all such a muddle. Maybe Dominic will be able to sort it all out. He could go and visit Lord Marchmont today and see if there is a chance he would sponsor us in society." Her spirits lifted at this thought, and she jumped out of bed prepared to enjoy the little time she did have to spend in London. "I think I will wear my flowered silk this morning, Annie, with only a small hoop. I intend to go out and see the sights, and I will have to walk if Dominic takes the carriage. You will not mind accompanying me, will you?"

"Oh no, Miss Sarah. Do you think we might see the king going into his palace?" The girl was pink with excitement.

Sarah laughed happily. "We only have to go just outside the door of this place to stare into St. James's Palace, Annie. I want to go farther afield than that."

"I do want to see the king before I go home again," Annie murmured, helping to arrange Sarah's petticoats.

Her mistress's face fell slightly at this mention of home, but she said nothing, not wishing to spoil her maid's pleasure. When Dominic at last ventured into his sister's chamber more than an hour later it was to find her with breakfast long finished and dressed ready for her walk in the April sunshine.

"May I speak to you, Sarah?" he asked hoarsely, averting his eyes from her smiling face.

"Of course you can, Dominic. I wanted to see you too, to suggest you visit Lord Marchmont this morning. He should have returned home, and you could make yourself known. He might be prepared to sponsor us, don't you think?" she said hopefully.

"No. He will do nothing for us, and nor would I ask him," Dominic snapped, forgetting for a moment the awful news he had to break to her.

"Have you met him already, then?" Sarah asked in surprise.

"Yes. Last night at the Cocoa Tree club," Dominic replied, and his voice dropped. He looked around desperately and saw Annie folding clothes over by the window. "Can you send Annie out for a few minutes? For I have something of a private nature to tell you."

Sarah took one look at his hunted expression and sent Annie on an errand, but her surprise deepened when Dominic dragged another young man into the room and shut the door behind him. "This is Jamie St. Clair. My sister, Sarah," he said, introducing them quickly. "He will verify what I am about to tell you, sis."

Sarah was puzzled rather than alarmed and wondered just what sort of scrape her brother had got into last night. She guessed the other young man was involved, and she sighed. Her brother had not really grown up yet, although he was twenty-one years old and three years her senior.

"What have you done now?" she said in some amusement. "Did you forget to come back here yesterday and spend the night in the open?"

What little that had been left of the night hours Dominic had spent in pacing his bedchamber wondering how he could tell his sister what he had done. In the early-morning light he had decided that he must have imagined most of what had happened, for even he

26

could never have done anything so dreadful as to use his sister for the stake in a bet. However, he had barely finished his breakfast when St. Clair had made his appearance, looking almost as bleary-eyed and even less cheerful. After a short conversation with him Dominic discovered he had indeed done all he had imagined and worse. What St. Clair couldn't remember for himself his valet had helpfully provided, for the story had spread all over town with appalling speed.

At first Dominic had been unable to believe it. "Surely I didn't do such a thing, Jamie?" he cried as his friend told the sad tale. "Don't you remember what really happened?"

Jamie shook his head miserably. "Sorry, old feller. 'Fraid I was in my cups a bit last night. I know we were playing with Hawkeworth and Marchmont—terrible feller, that—must have been him who spread it around, I suppose."

"I think I told him as I left the club," Dominic muttered, with a hollow feeling inside.

"Pity," Jamie remarked. "Much better if you had said nothing. Maybe we could have hushed it up then. Hawkeworth won't want your sister, after all. He's dangling after Delia Masterson. He could be very annoyed with you about this," he added—rather unhelpfully, Dominic thought.

He groaned. "Oh, Jamie! I must tell Sarah what has happened. What will she do?"

"Have hysterics, I expect," said his friend gloomily. "In my experience females always do, or else cry."

"Sarah never cries."

"Doesn't she? Lucky for you, old chap. Still, I thought I'd better come around and tell you what the tattle-mongers are saying right away. You could skip town, I suppose," he mused as the idea struck him.

Dominic shook his head. "How can I? This is a debt of honour. Will he call me out for it, do you think?"

Jamie pondered for a few minutes. "No. I doubt it.

After all, you offered your sister and the bet was laid and he won. Can't see what he can object to in that. Good thing really, since he's an excellent shot and good with a sword."

"If I refuse to honour my bet, though," Dominic suggested tentatively. "What would he do then?"

"You can't. You've just said as much. Debt of honour," protested Jamie. "Anyway, your sister wouldn't want you killed, would she? Better tell her and see."

Dominic held his head in his hands and groaned. "You must come with me, Jamie, and tell her it's true. Otherwise she'll think I've made the whole story up as a joke."

"Funny sort of joke," St. Clair said in a puzzled way. "Are you sure you want me to accompany you? Thought I'd look in on old George and see if he's recovered from last night. We could meet later," he suggested hopefully, edging toward the door.

A hand shot out and Dominic grasped his arm firmly. "Don't desert me, Jamie. I tell you she will never believe me unless someone tells her the tale is true. Would you believe it in her place?"

Thus questioned, St. Clair was forced to acknowledge Dominic's argument, and he reluctantly agreed to go along. So it was Sarah faced the two of them and thought they both resembled nothing more than a pair of schoolboys caught stealing apples.

"What happened last night?" she said again as Dominic fidgeted about and seemed afraid to speak.

"We went to the Cocoa Tree club for a spot of gaming," he managed at last. "I won quite a bit at first," he added, seeing her face. "But then my luck changed and I began to lose. Finally I made a win-or-lose-all bet with the gentleman who held my vowels, and he won." He stopped and looked wildly around for help from St. Clair.

"How much did he win?" Sarah prompted, all amusement gone now from her voice and face. "Have you lost all the money we had, Dominic?"

He nodded miserably. "And my horses and carriage—everything."

Sarah looked at St. Clair for confirmation, and he nodded his head too. "Then there is nothing for it. We must return to Sussex at once and hope brother Thomas will be generous," she said, striving for a light tone.

"There is worse to come," Dominic muttered. "I lost everything, including you."

"Me? Whatever are you talking about?" Sarah said. She began to feel worried that Dominic's folly had made him ill. "You cannot lose me, for I am not yours to lose," she said placatingly, as if to a child.

"But I did. I am your brother, head of our family, and I made a bet with you as stake, and I lost." Dominic had finally got it out.

At first Sarah could hardly comprehend what she had heard. She gazed from one man to the other, but neither would meet her eyes. "You cannot have done," she repeated and sat down on the nearest chair. "You cannot lose your sister in a bet. You must be mad to have suggested such a thing. Surely no gentleman took you seriously?"

"The Marquess of Hawkeworth always takes his bets seriously," Jamie put in earnestly. "He seemed to think nothing of it."

"Then he must have been mad or drunk," snapped Sarah. "I have never heard such rubbish. I know you gentlemen think a great deal about gambling and stupid bets, but I have never heard anything as silly as this. What do you propose to do now? Hand me over to him?"

"I must," Dominic muttered unhappily. "He is bound to treat you well, don't you think, Jamie?"

Before that young man could say anything, Sarah stood up and in spite of her lack of inches withered them both with her scorn. "He will not have the opportunity to treat me well or ill, I assure you. I am not a party to such nonsense and will not permit you to hand me over to anyone. I suppose you expect me to become his mistress quite tamely, do you?" she spat. "You must be as crazy as he is. I tell you if I meet him I'll show him what I think of betting with a girl as stake and he will regret his folly. Now get out of my way. I intend to see the sights of the town, but you had better make preparations for our return to Sussex. There is nothing else for us to do now. I will see you later when I return, and I hope by then you will have forgotten this madness."

Ignoring St. Clair completely, she swept from the room and down the stairs, gathering Annie up in her wake as she passed the servant on the stairs. So intent was she on leaving the Thatched House Tavern as quickly as possible Sarah did not notice the two gentlemen coming in the front door, and the next moment found herself walking straight into the taller of the two.

With an impatient exclamation she pushed herself away and murmured a brief apology. However, instead of releasing her he merely held her at arm's length and studied her lovely face, still stormy from her quarrel with Dominic.

"Who have we here?" murmured Hawkeworth in some amusement. "Is she a tigress or just a spitting kitten, do you think, Peter?"

Sarah's temper, still high from her recent outburst, blazed forth again. "Unhand me, sir!" she snapped at him furiously. "I am a guest in this hotel and as such expect the other patrons to treat me with courtesy and respect, but no doubt you are just in from the street!"

Hawkeworth dropped her arm at once and swept her a bow. He found her fury amusing and not a little tantalizing. Here was no milk-and-water maiden simpering at him but a woman of feeling and passion, yet so dainty and delicate she had passed him by before his bow was completed. Unused to such a deliberate snub delivered so publicly, Hawkeworth frowned and grasped the arm of the maid about to follow her mistress from the inn.

"What is the name of the lady who accidentally bumped into me?" he demanded fiercely.

"Miss Sarah Davenant, if you please, sir," Annie murmured. She dropped him a quick curtsy and fled, leaving the marquess staring after them both.

"So that is your lucky bet, Gerry," Sir Peter chuckled in his ear. "How do you feel about winning her now? Still full of chivalrous feelings, I hope."

The marquess shot him a look of dislike and walked on into the hotel, pausing only to inquire the direction of Mr. Davenant's rooms from a serving maid before disappearing up the stairs.

Chapter 4

Sarah had fled so precipitately from the hotel that Annie had difficulty catching up with her. When at last the maid managed to reach her her mistress had already traversed half St. James's Street and seemed bent on moving as fast as possible.

"Miss Sarah, do wait for me," Annie begged breathlessly. "I can't keep up with you. Wait. Please."

Realizing the maid's distress, Sarah slowed down, and gradually Annie recovered herself and her plump face took on a less red hue.

"I'm sorry, Annie. I was upset, and bumping into that impudent gentleman was just too much for me," Sarah apologized quickly. "But I had no wish to make you run so to keep up with me, and in fact I doubt if I could manage such a pace myself for long," she admitted.

"Where are we going, Miss Sarah?" Annie asked. She was a little disappointed that they had rushed off in the opposite direction to the Palace of St. James's, for she was determined to try to catch a glimpse of his majesty King George II before returning to Sussex.

Sarah paused for a moment and stood irresolute. Then she came to a decision. She still had a little money of her own, and this was probably her only chance of spending it on what she wanted. So, refusing to think of the future, she turned to her maid. "We will take a hackney carriage and go into the city. I would love to see St. Paul's Church, and afterward we can browse among the shops along Cheapside. Would you like that?"

"Oh yes, Miss Sarah," Annie breathed, her face glowing with pleasure. "That will be something to tell my folks, and Edward will be real envious of me."

Feeling slightly more cheerful at Annie's delighted reaction, Sarah managed to secure a hackney carriage for them and gave directions to the driver. She was unable to suppress her own feelings of excitement, and as the carriage rolled along Piccadilly and down the Haymarket and passed the imposing portals of Northumberland House she had almost put her quarrel with her brother out of her mind. The ridiculous bet he had made she had already dismissed as nonsense, for in this enlightened age nobody could expect to take such things seriously. As the bustle of the streets unfolded in front of them Sarah did find herself wondering who the darkly handsome gentleman she had walked into was. He had been taller than average and of a striking appearance, dressed with a quiet elegance that normally she would have admired. His rudeness and her own temper had made her perhaps hasty in her treatment of him, and she grew rather hot with embarrassment at the remembrance of the scene; but then she was not in the habit of being held out for inspection nor of being referred to in that odious way as a "spitting kitten." Her eyes sparkled again at the very idea, and she dismissed her fleeting interest in his person as quite unworthy and concentrated instead on catching a good view of the imposing archway of Temple Bar as the coach rattled over the ruts and cobbles beneath it.

Dominic would have envied his sister her ability to dismiss Hawkeworth from her mind so easily. He had barely recovered some measure of calm after her disastrous outburst before he had had to face that gentleman in person. In fact, the knock on the door occurred just as he was mulling over with St. Clair what he could do about the whole sorry tangle.

"Sarah doesn't seem to realize a bet is a serious matter," he groaned in Jamie's sympathetic ear. "How can I possibly make her understand? She just dismissed it all as nonsense. Do you think Hawkeworth will do the same?" His countenance brightened hopefully but fell at St. Clair's words.

"He might have last night, but not now," that young man commented thoughtfully. "Stands to reason he can't, since the whole town will be talking about it tonight. He must do something or stand to look a fool, and he would never do that."

"What can I do then? I suppose I could enlist and disappear before he comes to see me," Dominic suggested without much enthusiasm. "I don't suppose Sarah will be sorry if I'm killed in a battle or something."

St. Clair was about to agree that she might even welcome his demise in her present mood when the knock fell on the door. Dominic winced visibly, and Jamie put a hand to his aching head and slipped over to stand by the window almost hidden from view.

"Come in," called Dominic weakly, hoping it was only a servant or even Sarah again with a change of heart.

He was unlucky. The door swept open and the marquess walked in, followed moments later by Sir Peter Trevenning. Hawkeworth ran his eye around the room, noted the disorder and the cringing figure of St. Clair by the window, and flicked his glance back to Davenant. He sighed. This whole business had turned from an evening's entertainment and a little joke to what was now rapidly assuming the proportions of a nightmare. How could he have been so stupid as to suggest a lighthearted bet to get this wretched young man out of his difficulties? "I should always stick to my own policy of thinking of nothing but myself," he murmured in an undertone.

Dominic heard him and looked startled, while Trevenning permitted himself a slight grin, for he knew Hawkeworth's frequently pronounced philosophy of self, which was often belied by his actions when he was unlikely to be discovered. However, this was certainly no matter for amusement, and Trevenning grew grave again almost at once.

Hawkeworth strode into the center of the room and flicked his gloves idly to and fro before placing them with his cane and three-cornered hat of black silk on the nearby table. "You were expecting me?" he said calmly. "Perhaps you would be so good as to introduce me to your sister." Since he knew exactly where Miss Sarah Davenant was at that moment, which was more than Dominic did, he waited with veiled interest to see what would happen next.

Trevenning frowned slightly, for he too had heard who the lady was who had swept out of the hotel and he did not approve of this levity, but he held his tongue.

"My sister is—well, she is indisposed at present," Dominic blurted out hurriedly.

Hawkeworth's eyebrows rose. "Oh dear! How very unfortunate. In the circumstances I hoped to view my new acquisition. May I ask if the news of her good fortune prostrated her?"

Trevenning coughed reproachfully and shot his friend a look of irritation which the marquess ignored. St. Clair managed to worm his way behind the heavy curtains and prayed they would forget about him while Dominic stood, scarlet-faced, and tried to think of an answer.

"She is prostrate, I suppose?" Hawkeworth repeated as Davenant said nothing.

"Ah! Well, I think so. That is, I don't really know. She, well, she just walked out when I told her," he stated baldly.

"It would seem her good fortune did go to her head," Trevenning could not help saying.

The marquess's expression lightened and he grinned at his old friend. "Your point, I think, Peter. However, I must ask when I am going to receive your sister, or should I say if I am going to receive her. Would that be the better way around it?"

Dominic gulped visibly and loosened his cravat in an attempt to breathe more easily. "She was distraught," he got out eventually. "Had to lie down to recover. Nerves, you know. Female sensibility and all that. It was rather a shock, you see, and she is only a little thing and so couldn't take it all in, and her maid is with her," he finished. He hoped this explanation would suffice, but he disliked the wicked gleam in the marquess's eyes.

"Part of that rigamarole is indeed correct, I'm sure, Davenant, although I had difficulty following such a story," he remarked with heavy irony. "I am uncertain what I should do about a female of sensibility, though. Do you think one who is so afflicted at the thought of me will suit me after all?" he asked Trevenning with genuine interest.

Trevenning was having difficulty preventing himself from saying something and he was now forced to retire behind his handkerchief. He was annoyed with Hawkeworth for treating this with such lightness, for indeed the whole situation was an unhappy one.

"I know, Peter. You despair of me, don't you?" Hawkeworth said sympathetically. "But if I don't attempt to get some amusement from this—this farce—I fear I shall be forced to take violent action."

"Farce? It is hardly a farce for me, my lord, nor for my poor sister," Dominic said indignantly, his own woes forgotten for the moment. "I cannot understand all you say, but I know you are making fun of me. Well, that may be all right for you, but my sister was horrified, as well she might be. So I ask you now, can I

36

pay you a further sum to keep my sister out of the matter entirely?"

"Your sentiments do you credit, although belatedly," Hawkeworth said smoothly, but now there was a hint of anger in his tone. "I cannot imagine why horror should be your sister's emotion at the thought of me. Most women swoon at my attentions."

"Not Sarah," Dominic retorted. "She would never swoon for any man, whoever he was."

The marquess thought this very likely from the brief glimpse he had been privileged to enjoy of Miss Davenant, and her brother's comments only intrigued him more. Maybe something worthwhile could be salvaged from the mess after all. "Her sentiments are not important anyway," Hawkeworth said in dismissal. "I cannot allow you to pay me to keep her name out of it. That is quite impossible."

"Why?" Dominic burst out wretchedly. "Surely you don't want my sister, and I will pay you anything you like."

"What with, I wonder," Sir Peter drawled softly for the marquess's ears alone.

Sighing, Hawkeworth nodded. "It is not a matter of money, I fear," he said somewhat grimly. "Maybe last night I would have accepted your proposal, for you are quite right—I have no wish to be saddled with your sister; she will not fit into my plans at all. However, it is now a matter of honour, my honour, and yours, although I admit that is of no interest to me."

"I will fight you if you like. You can choose your weapons," Dominic said desperately and ignored the exclamation of horror from behind the curtains.

Trevenning heard it and had to smother another laugh. There was no doubt of it; Gerry was right—it was a farce.

"You must see what a stupid suggestion that is," the marquess said softly. "I have not insulted you, so there is no reason for you to demand satisfaction even if I was prepared to give it to you, and I have no wish to give you a reason for similar satisfaction. I feel myself the wronged party if anyone is, although I was foolish enough to propose the bet in the first place."

"But I suggested my sister as a stake, so the fault is mine," Dominic admitted honestly.

Hawkeworth sighed again. The pup was honourable, and that made it all the more difficult.

"Do you have to go through with it?" Dominic asked. "Is there no way out for my sister?"

"Can you suggest one?" the marquess parried.

"You could both leave the country," Sir Peter Trevenning put in quickly. This idea was his own, but it had found favor with Hawkeworth when he had mentioned it as a solution. Particularly if Hawkeworth returned the lad's money and vowels as he had said he would. The two of them could stay away for six months until the affair blew over. But Trevenning saw that Hawkeworth made no move to endorse his suggestion, although Davenant looked hopeful. What was his devil of a friend planning now?

"Could we do that?" Dominic said, barely concealing the eager tremor in his voice.

"A possible answer if you have sufficient funds," the marquess mused. "You can never return if your obligations are not met first, though," he added significantly and refused to meet Trevenning's eyes.

"I shall have to sell everything I have if I am to pay you my other debts," Dominic said quietly. "That means we cannot flee even if Sarah would agree."

"You think she would not?" the marquess asked.

"She refuses even to recognize that I owe such a debt to you. Said I had no right to suggest such a thing and you must have been mad to take up the challenge," he muttered without thinking.

St. Clair's groan made Dominic aware of his mistake, and even Trevenning could have kicked the young man for his tactlessness. Nothing would be more likely to arouse Hawkeworth's interest, and one look at his face proved that it had.

"Ah! I see. I'm mad as well as rude. Your sister intrigues me. I think I shall dine below and await her return," Hawkeworth said cheerfully.

"Her return? Has she gone out?" Dominic asked.

"Oh dear! A slip of the tongue. I believe a servant did tell us on the way up that Miss Davenant had left the Thatched House Tavern," the marquess said blandly.

Dominic could face no more of this. He swallowed hard and drew himself up. "It is no good your waiting to see her, then, for she will have nothing to do with you. I think I must have been the mad one to suggest the stake I did, and I can only say I offer you my apologies and wish to retract it now. I will pay the money I owe, but my sister is not part of my folly. You must forget that last bet completely."

There was a stunned silence in the room. Behind the curtains St. Clair held his breath and waited for the explosion, and even Trevenning nerved himself to endure an outburst.

The marquess looked straight at Dominic and held his eyes for a few seconds before the young man's gaze fell. "I think I will just forget you said that at all," Hawkeworth murmured very softly. "It would be best for all of us. I admit that last night I only intended a joke when I accepted your bet, but things have gone far beyond that now. My name is being bandied around town in connection with your sister, who is now confidently expected to be under my protection. If for no other reason than notoriety alone I must do what is expected of me, since my name is already ruined in those quarters where it mattered, as you will soon realize if you didn't know before. A certain person has taken it upon himself to spread the entire tale around all the cream of society in London, and your sister will have to comply if any of us are to be saved from a monumental scandal. Ask your hidden friend if you don't believe me. You need have no fears for your sister, for I will not harm her, but mine she is from now onward. I will return this evening to collect her and her maid, so be sure she is ready."

He swept up his gloves, cane, and hat. At the door he paused again and looked at Dominic long and hard. "This may be a bitter introduction to society for you, but it is no less a bitter blow to my own hopes of happiness. Take this as a warning and in future keep your own counsel in all matters. You alone betrayed your sister when you opened your mouth and told the tale afterward, otherwise it need never have gone beyond these four walls. Here," he added, dipping into his coat pocket. "I think you will find these are all your vowels and gold from your play last night. I never take money from a member of the family." With this he walked out, and Trevenning followed.

Chapter 5

When the two men were alone once more, St. Clair edged himself out from behind the curtains and wiped his brow. His wig was disordered from his concealment, but he was not interested in his appearance.

"We need a drink badly," he said and moved to the bell rope. With a nervous tug he jerked the rope several times and did not move again until the servant entered and had been dispatched to bring bottles and glasses on the double.

"Why has he given me these?" Dominic asked. He riffled through the vowels and notes in front of him and idly added up the total. His shock at the sum was so great that when the wine arrived he drained a glass straight off in his horror. "Do you realize he has handed me back money and notes for over a thousand pounds?"

St. Clair was almost as amazed but could understand the reasoning better than his companion. "He told you why he gave them back," he murmured, starting on a second glass. "Going to be a member of the family, and he can't take money from you." He relaxed in the chair and filled the glass up for the third time.

Dominic pushed his own empty one away and gazed at St. Clair as if he had turned into a monster.

"Become a member of his family! What does he mean?"

"When he marries your sister, of course," Jamie explained kindly. "Lucky girl, you know. He's very rich and has been been dangling after the lovely Delia."

"So you said last night. Do you think he means it, then? He intends to marry Sarah?"

Jamie sat up with a jerk and spilled some of the wine down his beige twill coat. He cursed in dismay and dabbed ineffectually at the spreading stain with a wisp of lace. "Look at that! Ruined! And this is the first wearing. I was particularly pleased with the cut of the coattails, which swing out when I walk. Don't get agitated," he added as Dominic thumped the table in irritation at this inconsequential chatter. "Of course he will marry your sister. I said so, didn't I? What did you expect him to do? Make her his mistress? Very unlikely, old boy, for his taste runs to more mature ladies with—well—" He sketched a figure in the air. "With generous curves," he finished cheerfully. "But whatever he does to please himself, at least your sister will share his name and fortune. Be the making of you too," he added.

Instead of feeling happy, this news served to plunge Dominic into the deepest gloom. "I don't want to be beholden to my sister's husband," he muttered petulantly. "At least I don't think I do."

"Why not?" said his friend sensibly.

"It's no good. Sarah will never marry him."

"She'll have to," Jamie said, sounding happy now that the wine was coursing through him. "Only way to sort the matter out and avoid scandal. Hawkeworth won't have scandal attached to his name. He's very particular even if he is a bit of a rake. But with his money nobody minds how he conducts himself as long as he's discreet."

"Sarah will." Dominic was still depressed. "She will never agree. I tell you, I know my sister. She has some odd notion that people should marry for love or some

42

such twaddle. Anyway, she will never marry this man because of the bet."

"That's the very reason she has to—on account of the bet," Jamie insisted. He sat up and poured Dominic another glass. "Drink up and forget these gloomy thoughts. Any girl in her right mind would take the Marquess of Hawkeworth. Why, there are dozens of mamas in London who would fall over themselves, and their daughters as well. She will be the most envied girl in town."

This view cheered Dominic slightly but failed to reassure him, for he knew Sarah and St. Clair did not. Even a few more glasses of wine and an excellent meal of all the best dishes the Thatched House Tavern could produce did not change his mind, and when Sarah returned she confirmed his worst forebodings.

He waited until she had partaken of a good meal and described her day's sightseeing in detail before broaching the subject, but his forbearance did no good. When she was ready to talk she launched straight into her own plans without giving him a chance to put his own point first.

"Have you arranged for us to leave town for Sussex tomorrow?" she asked at once. They were both seated in the private parlor he had obtained, for which seclusion he was very grateful. "If not I would enjoy another day looking around London, for I have not visited Westminster Abbey yet and Annie is still determined to see the king. But if the arrangements have been made I am happy enough to go."

"I thought we could stay for a little longer," Dominic began, but she interrupted him before he went any further.

"I cannot help you to pay the bills here," she said firmly. "I hope you have sufficient funds left after your disastrous evening to do so. Can you afford another night or two?"

"Certainly," he said stiffly. "I have plenty of money.

Look," he added rashly, tipping the gold sovereigns he had been given earlier into her lap.

Sarah looked at the glittering heap in silence, and when she faced him again he could see the familiar signs of a storm about to break on her face.

"It's all right," he said quickly. "This is my own money. Lord Hawkeworth gave me back all my vowels and the gold he won off me, so I don't have to sell anything. I can even keep my horses and the carriage."

Her face cleared and she relaxed. "I thought all that you talked about this morning was nonsense. No decent gentleman would take so much money from a flat like you. It wouldn't be fair."

"Sarah! I am not a flat, and where did you pick up such an expression anyway?" Dominic was outraged.

She giggled. "Annie used it to describe a young man who had got into debt. I didn't tell her what you had done, although I expect Edward will if he knows. They are going to get married when we have settled our own future. Did you know?"

Dominic was diverted for a moment from the news he had to give her. "Is that so? Why, I think they will suit very well. What a pity we are not still living in our old home. The coachhouse flat would have made a good place for them, and I always felt Edward was a better groom than a valet."

"Judging from your appearance I agree with you," Sarah retorted. "Still, we couldn't bring more than one servant apiece, and Edward and Annie are devoted to us as well as each other. Let's hope now you have your money again we can sort out something for ourselves. Have you thought about the possibility of approaching Lord Marchmont again?"

Knowing as he did that the peer had been the cause of most of his troubles by the way he had spread around the story of the foolish bet, Dominic could only grind his teeth with rage. "I have no intention of applying to that little viper," he told her. "He is a detestable fop."

"Oh dear. That is a pity. Never mind. We will find a way out, I expect. Now I think I will go to bed, as I'm rather tired."

Sarah got up, but Dominic had risen before her in alarm. "You can't go to bed yet!" he exclaimed. "It's still early."

"I suppose it is, but I'm tired," Sarah said in surprise. "I have been on the go all day."

The realization that the marquess might arrive any minute and he had still not explained the position filled Dominic with fresh dread. "You can't go to bed," he stammered. "You must wait and meet the Marquess of Hawkeworth. He is coming around to see you shortly."

"To see me? Why?" she demanded. Her face was flushed now and she looked very pretty with her unpowdered curls bobbing in disarray.

Dominic was in no mood to appreciate beauty, especially his sister's. "He insists I keep to my bet of last night and will not settle for less. He intends coming here to meet you, but he does mean to marry you, at least."

"You are not serious, Dominic?" she questioned softly, clutching the chair back to conceal the sudden trembling in her hands. "He gave you your money back. You said so. Surely that means the whole business is over and done with?"

"No, it isn't. It's all over town how I bet with you as my stake and lost, and now you are his property, and for that we have to thank the gossiping tongue of Lord Marchmont," he shouted bitterly. He omitted to mention how he had told Marchmont in the first place, but Sarah's white face was bad enough.

"It can't be true," she whispered. "This is 1752. People don't bet with the lives of other human beings in this day. You must be mistaken—you have to be!"

"It would have been different if nobody knew about it, but now the whole affair is a matter of honour—his and mine. You cannot let our family down, Sarah. I would be ruined forever," Dominic cried in anguish.

She was almost persuaded by the desperation she saw in his face. Then she thought of an unknown man tied to her for life, all for the sake of some stupid bet and the gentleman's code of honour. It was beyond bearing.

"I cannot marry a man I don't know and don't care for," she exclaimed. "Why, he might be old and ugly, and he must be crazy to think of this at all. He cannot want to marry me."

"No, he doesn't. He was courting the beauty Delia Masterson, so Jamie tells me. But he has to marry you to silence the gossip and keep his own honour and family name clear of scandal, and mine. Anyway, he is not old, only about twenty-eight, nor ugly. He is so rich you will be doing well for yourself," he finished on a more sulky note. "Jamie said you would be the envy of London."

"I would prefer to be hated by all and have my name dragged in the mire before being a party to such a plan," she spat at him recklessly.

"Would you indeed, Miss Davenant?" drawled a voice from the doorway. "It is a pity I cannot permit you to act as foolishly as you like and as your brother already has done, but then I have a care for my name, which is why I am here."

Both the brother and sister spun around at once to see Hawkeworth lounging in the doorway. He was dressed for the evening in a dark-red silk coat with paler-colored breeches. His heavily embroidered gold waistcoat was fashionably short, and Sarah noticed the lace at his wrists and throat was very fine. If she had not been so shocked to see who it was she would have admired him as she had done in their brief encounter earlier, but that this should be the man her brother had been talking about was too terrible.

"Not you," she whispered in accents of loathing.

"I am the Marquess of Hawkeworth, and your brother has undoubtedly told you all about me," he replied, a slight smile curling the corners of his mouth. "You are still the little tigress, I see, and I am still the man from the street."

She was not cowed by this reference, but her cheeks grew rosy, and he thought how lovely she looked with her green eyes sparkling at him. He might well be getting a bargain after all.

"I have no wish to meet you, sir, nor do I intend to have anything further to do with you," Sarah said. She drew herself up to her full height but was scarcely as high as his shoulder. Her lack of inches made her feel at a disadvantage for once, and she refused to admit, even to herself, that this man was one of the most handsome and dangerous she had ever met.

The marquess looked over to Dominic. "I hope you realized what I meant this morning and explained the position to your sister."

"I think so, but I'm not sure," he faltered.

"Then I had better do so again," Hawkeworth said patiently. "Miss Davenant," he began and bowed courteously. "I am sorry to disappoint you, but you are about to become my wife and as such the mistress of my not inconsiderable household. I can see that this does not please you, but for all our sakes it is the sensible course of action for us to take, and I hope you will grow accustomed to the idea."

"Never," she flashed at him contemptuously. "I will never marry you." She turned her back on him and stared defiantly at the closed curtains over the window.

Fury showed briefly in the marquess's expression, for he was not used to rebuffs of any kind. He resisted the desire to cross the room and turn her around forcibly to face him. Instead he rounded on her brother. "I see you did not explain the position at all satisfactorily. As your sister refuses to acknowledge my presence, I will discuss the details with you. I will not be ungenerous to you both, and if you wish for references, any one of my dozens of friends and acquaintances will furnish you with an account of my wealth and social standing in the town. No doubt when your sister learns I am a rich man she will regard me with more favor and become more amenable," he sneered.

At this Sarah whipped around as he had guessed she would. Scorn filled her face and voice as she snapped back. "I want nothing to do with you and even less with your riches. To discuss money in front of me is both vulgar and ill-bred. I thought you were a gentleman who cared for social niceties. Why else are you prepared to go through with this farce?"

Unconsciously she echoed his own term of earlier in the day, and he was reminded of it forcibly. He wished she would look less fierce and that he already had the right to tame her, but this was not a moment to show any softness.

"You will marry me, Miss Davenant. Tonight."

For a moment Sarah paused as his words sank into her brain. Then she whirled around and made for the door. "I will never marry you willingly. You will have to drag me to the altar, for I will not go there otherwise."

He caught hold of her arm as she passed him, pulling her back and bruising the flesh. "I say you will marry me tonight, Miss Davenant, so prepare yourself. Your brother has given his consent, you are underage, and you will be my bride like it or not." He flung her away. "I will give you one hour to get ready. I will wait for you both below." With that he turned on his heel and left them alone.

Sarah looked at Dominic, saw his irresolution, and knew he would side with the marquess. If she wanted to save herself she had to rely on her own wits. With a stifled sob she ran from the room and rushed into her own chamber, slamming the door behind her.

Chapter 6

Once again Annie was startled out of a doze in front of the fire. On seeing how distraught her mistress was she rushed across and led her to the chair, then busied herself preparing the hot posset she had left warming by the fire.

After a few minutes Sarah calmed down a little and began to think. She could hardly believe the speed with which these misfortunes had overtaken both herself and her brother. They had not been in London two days before Dominic had plunged them into the most impossible situation, far worse than any of his earlier scrapes back home in Sussex. How she wished they could return to that quiet, peaceful life which they had enjoyed before her father's untimely death. Even the dullness of that routine would be welcome in preference to the problems she now faced.

Annie proffered the hot drink, but Sarah waved it away. She wanted to keep her wits about her, for the only solution seemed to lie in her leaving the Thatched House Tavern and keeping out of sight until the marquess forgot the whole affair. She was certain that this type of story would be of interest for only a few days, and when society had something else to talk about the silly bet would be forgotten. If she disappeared he could not marry her and Dominic could not be forced into helping him, for there could be no marriage without a bride.

Having reached this conclusion, Sarah decided she would have to take Annie into her confidence in order to leave the hotel undetected. She quickly explained what had been happening, and the maid's eyes grew round with wonder.

"Oh Miss Sarah! Fancy you marrying a marquess!" she exclaimed with a happy grin on her face. "I never thought that would happen when we left Sussex."

"And it's not going to take place now, you silly girl," Sarah cried in exasperation. "I don't want to marry the man, and I will be forced to if I stay here. You must help me escape from this hotel without anyone seeing me go."

"You don't want to marry him?" Annie could hardly believe it. "Why not, Miss Sarah? He's ever so handsome, and if your brother says he is rich as well, what more could you want?"

What more indeed, Sarah wondered briefly, her thoughts turning to the mocking face and well-set figure of the dashing marquess. If she had met him in different circumstances, if she had not been used in such a fashion, why then it might have been different. But—and here she stopped herself. It was no use dreaming of what could have been. She had to get away and avoid this marriage at all costs. No gentleman's name would be ruined if she disappeared, she argued to herself, and anyway this marquess wanted to marry someone else, so Dominic said. If she could not be found, then he would be able to do so after a decent interval had elapsed. She tried to explain something of this to Annie, but the girl seemed disappointed in her mistress's decision and failed to appreciate her sentiments.

Since Annie was clearly only thinking how romantic

it all was, Sarah pondered on the advisibility of taking her along too. She had intended to leave with Annie and seek sanctuary with old Nanny for a few weeks until she could decently return to Sussex. Now it seemed as if Annie might betray them, for her heart was not in it, and she would miss Edward or maybe even tell him something before they left which would ruin her plans. So Sarah refused to explain where she intended to go.

"I just want you to lend me your oldest clothes, Annie. You needn't worry, for I will return them to you eventually. Then you must put on one of my gowns and stay here with your back to the door. If Dominic comes looking for me, he will imagine I am sitting by the fire, which may give me a little more time. Run along and get your things. Be quick now, for I have only an hour, and in that time I must get out of the hotel and be far away."

Annie was able to enter into this part of the conspiracy with enthusiasm. She returned in a very few minutes with the necessary clothes and helped her mistress shed her silks and slip into the heavy clumsy cottons of her own working garments with great glee.

"Your hair gives you away, Miss Sarah," she said, standing back to survey their efforts. "And your shoes. I never wear fine slippers like those you have on," she added with a sigh.

A quick look in the mirror showed Sarah that Annie was right. It was with some reluctance that she took off her own soft kid shoes and put on the much heavier ones that Annie wore every day. While the maid dressed up in silks and preened herself in her mistress's finery, Sarah brushed her hair free of powder and changed the formal arrangement of her ringlets for a tumbled mass of curls surrounding her face. When she had covered her head with a frilly white cotton cap she did indeed look very different. A little dirt on her cheeks completed her transformation, and her spirits began to rise as the moment for escape came nearer.

"I will take the glass and the tray back to the kitchens as if I were a maid, and then I can slip out the rear of the inn and be away before anyone has missed me," Sarah said in a brighter tone. She tucked her purse into her waist and threw a shawl around her shoulders. "You sit here until my brother comes and tell him nothing. Don't worry, for he will not be upset with you."

"Where be you going, Miss Sarah?" Annie asked, her face crinkling now the moment of parting had come. "I should be with you. 'Tain't right for a lady to wander the streets alone, and in London at that."

"I shall be all right. I intend to take a hackney as soon as I can, and I have money, so I will be able to pay for what I need. It is the best way. Believe me."

Sarah picked up the tray with the glass and the full jug of the posset still on it. She opened her door a crack and peered out. Seeing the corridor was empty, she slipped out, and Annie closed the door behind her. Now Sarah was on her own, and instead of turning toward the stairs for the guests leading to the front of the hotel she made her way to the twisting back stairs and clattered down the uncarpeted treads, wishing the heavy shoes made less noise. Below was the bustle of a busy tavern, and waiters pushed past her carrying platters of food, jugs, and bottles while harassed maids strove to answer all the demands made by the clientele.

It was not difficult to find a door out into the yard, and Sarah only had to avoid the rushing figures and the shouts for her to give a hand. She found she was still carrying the tray as she reached the nearest door and was glad when an ostler opened it, and as he entered she thrust the posset at him and disappeared into the yard beyond.

The night air was fresh, and she was glad of the shawl to pull round her shoulders. Although it was

April it still grew very chilly in the evening, and the yard was deep in mud and straw. Men moved in the shadows and horses neighed from the stables opposite. The large shape of a coach stood to one side, and an elegant chaise was standing lit by the blaze of many lanterns while ostlers worked quickly to change the horses.

Skirting the mud and filth in the middle of the yard, Sarah stayed as near the walls as she could and moved around toward the street entrance. She had to pass several lighted windows and hoped that the Marquess of Hawkeworth was not inside looking out, although she thought he was unlikely to recognize her.

If she had known it, Sir Peter Trevenning did catch sight of her as she slipped past. He was just settling down to enjoy a bottle of good burgundy with his friend before joining the wedding party to witness the marriage as he had promised he would. The face of the girl who flitted quickly past outside awoke a chord in his memory, but her servant's cap confused him, and he turned back to try to cheer Hawkeworth, forgetting the momentary glimpse he had had.

"Do you really need to go through with this wedding?" he asked in a low voice. He had no wish for anyone sitting at the neighboring tables to overhear his conversation.

Hawkeworth nodded his head. "If I marry her tonight, then we can spread the story abroad tomorrow of our romantic wedding and the joke her brother played by giving me her hand in the form of a bet. From a scandal the story will be transformed overnight into the sickly rubbish so beloved by the twittering ladies of fashion." His brooding glance rested on the bottle, but he made no effort to drink his glass of wine.

"You sound bitter. Will you really have any chance of happiness by entering into a marriage in this way?" Trevenning asked in concern. He had intended to be cheerful, but he was worried by the marquess's unaccustomed silence. If he had known that Hawkeworth was not thinking of the future with dismay but of the challenge this bride would offer and of her flashing eyes and dainty person, he might have been less upset.

Hawkeworth stared at Trevenning thoughtfully. "I suppose a marriage such as this will stand an even chance," he murmured. "If I had been successful in winning the hand of the beautiful Delia Masterson would I have been any happier once she was my wife?"

"I doubt it. She is an empty-headed creature and only the reigning toast because of her incredible fair hair and pink-and-white complexion," said Sir Peter brutally.

"Exactly so. Maybe in fact I shall have begun my revenge on Marchmont by allowing him to make the running and win her himself." He laughed in genuine amusement. "I could well be sparing myself countless years of boredom, for I don't believe this Davenant chit will prove a quiet and amenable wife."

"More likely just the opposite," said Trevenning. "Forget it all, Gerry, and give the ton a few days to find another tale to tattle about. It will all blow over soon enough."

"I shall not be able to win the Masterson, though," the marquess reminded him.

"Not her, no. But as you have said yourself, she would bore you inside a week. I think you only began to dangle after her because it was the thing to do and because Marchmont fancied his chances."

The marquess's eyes gleamed. "How well you know me, Peter. But enough of this talk. I have allowed that pair more than an hour. It is time we collected them."

"Are you sure you wish to be allied to the family?" Trevenning said, trying one last hope.

The marquess was already on his feet, and he looked down at his friend with amusement. "Oh, the Davenant family is good enough, even for me. Their pedigree is excellent and goes back farther than yours. They are just penniless, or almost."

"Yet you said she scorned you and your wealth?" Trevenning stood up and did nothing to conceal his amazement.

"As I said, life will not be dull with Miss Sarah Davenant. Now we must go. I have the licence procured from my reluctant brother-in-law, the bishop. He does not approve but prefers to legalize the union, so he told me."

"Gerry! He never said that!"

"Indeed he did," Hawkeworth murmured softly as they moved toward the stairs. "He dislikes my way of life and never ceases to tell me so. He has lent me his own chaplain to perform the ceremony, which shows he is anxious to reform me."

"Then for your sake I hope the bride is now willing. Bishop Turner will have lent you a prude like himself, and you will never drag a reluctant female in front of him."

Trevenning's last remark irritated the marquess, for he knew it to be true. It was the one source of annoyance about the whole business, although he found it far more intriguing to learn that a lady like Sarah Davenant could scorn his riches. In a few more moments he discovered that she had scorned him completely, for it took Dominic only a second to find the substitute in his sister's bedchamber.

Dominic was more alarmed by the reaction to Sarah's flight than he had been to the idea of the marriage. He took one look at the grim and furious face of the Marquess of Hawkeworth when he told him she had fled and found himself stammering incoherently just like a schoolboy.

"Stop giving me these excuses and tell me where she has gone," thundered the marquess. "I will find her if it takes me all night."

"I don't know, my lord," Dominic muttered.

"Then ask her maid."

Annie was soon reduced to tears by the icy politeness and fury of Hawkeworth, and it took all Trevenning's tact to elicit the information they wanted. When she had told them all she knew, which was very little, Trevenning turned back to Dominic.

"Where do you think she will have gone?" he asked quietly. "It would be much better for us all if you tell Hawkeworth now."

"I realize that," Dominic said, some of his normal assurance returning. "I don't like to think of her wandering alone in London."

"She said she had money and was going to hire a hackney carriage," Annie put in bravely.

"Then she must be setting off for our old home in Sussex to throw herself on Thomas's mercy," Dominic said quickly. "Thank God. I will go after her immediately and see if I can talk some sense into her."

"A good idea. Take your carriage and leave at once," the marquess ordered crisply. "Trevenning, go with him and see if your tact and persuasion cannot work wonders for us all with the poor girl."

Trevenning looked slightly baffled by Hawkeworth's sudden amiability, and he was faintly suspicious. Surely Gerry should go himself in pursuit of his bride. When he suggested this, Hawkeworth refused the idea at once.

"I must have frightened her earlier this evening," he explained. "If I chase after her I could well ruin everything. We must stick to our plan for marriage, but I must woo her," he said, turning a bland face toward his friend. "Don't you think that will be best?"

Trevenning nodded his head, for what the marquess said was perfectly reasonable. Still, he was not satisfied, although he agreed to accompany Davenant in his carriage. When he found that Hawkeworth had sent them both off without Davenant's groom cum valet in order to keep the chaise as light as possible to make for maximum speed, he was certain something was afoot; but by that time he was bowling along the Old Kent Road and could do little to prevent his friend from attempting something reckless.

Once Trevenning had set off with Davenant, the Marquess of Hawkeworth returned to the room in the Thatched House Tavern where he had left the two servants. The maid was still crying, but the young man, Edward, seemed more concerned with tidying up the mess left by his master.

"I think you know more about her disappearance than you said." Hawkeworth addressed Annie but watched Edward's face for any telltale sign.

"No, my lord. Really, I don't know where she went. She wouldn't tell me 'cos she said I didn't understand and it wasn't romantic or anything like that," Annie sniffed.

Hiding a smile, the marquess patted her hand absently. His real interest was Edward. "I think you have guessed her destination, and I want to know it," he said softly. "No lady would bother to change her clothes with her maid just to leave this hotel. I think she was going to another part of London where her fine silks would stand out. Am I right?" he rapped out.

"I did wonder about that meself, my lord," Edward admitted reluctantly. "I thought perhaps she had gone to seek shelter with old Nanny."

"Of course. That must be where she's gone," Annie exclaimed. "Why didn't I think of it before Master Dominic left? Do you think we can stop him going all the way to Lewes?"

"I doubt it," the marquess replied. "Anyway, the drive will do him good and cool his head." He was indifferent to Dominic's problems. "What I want to know is, where does this old Nanny of hers live? I would like you to tell me," he said, his manner now betraying nothing of the anger and irritation he had shown earlier. Instead he put himself out to charm the

57

two servants and had no difficulty in obtaining all the information he needed. He even agreed to take Annie with him and permitted Edward to direct him, since that young man had taken the old woman to her sister's cottage at Knightsbridge the day before.

It wanted only an hour to midnight when the odd trio set off with Edward driving the elegant chaise that Sarah had seen earlier in the yard of the tavern. The marquess had abandoned his groom without a qualm and sent him back to the Hawkeworth mansion in Grosvenor Square with messages for the waiting chaplain telling him his services were no longer required. The marquess had another reason for wanting none of his servants to discover exactly what went on, for he was fairly confident that he could ensure the silence of the Davenant retainers, particularly with the added inducement of pecuniary reward later. With no awkward witnesses to tell the truth he would be able to spread whatever story he liked next day and be believed by fashionable society.

With this in mind he sat back, reclining comfortably against the silken squabs, while Annie huddled herself into the corner opposite, for she was still much in awe of this great gentleman.

Chapter 7

It had taken Sarah precious moments to find her way out of the maze of alleys leading off behind the Thatched House Tavern. She had turned in the opposite direction from the main archway leading back into St. James's Street, fearing to run into the marquess or to look out of place in her servant's clothes in such a fashionable thoroughfare. However, the narrow and very dirty little passageway she trod only led her into several ill-smelling alleys until she found an opening leading into a larger and better-lit street. Her relief was great, for she had been afraid of attack from footpads and other wandering rogues who thronged the ill-lit back streets ready to pounce on unwary gentry who had missed their way.

Even when she reached Bury Street her troubles were not over. There was no sign of any hackney, and when she hailed a passing sedan chair hoping to get away from the area at least she was rudely told to be off, for the chairmen had no intention of soiling their silken sedan with the likes of her.

This was frightening, and Sarah was relieved when a wandering linkboy noticed her discomfiture and offered to walk with her to Piccadilly. "Wanting a 'ackney then, love?" he asked. "Where be you off to, then? If 'tis not far I'll light yer way for a shillun." He grinned impudently, and Sarah smiled back.

"I do want to find a hackney carriage," she admitted quickly. "Can you light me to the nearest place where I can find one?"

The scruffy lad paused and eyed her more closely. She pulled her shawl around her face, hoping he would stop his inspection. After holding his light, which was a torch of flaming pitch, over her head and taking in her appearance closely, he nodded. "Orlright then," he agreed gruffly. "Fancy ladies' maid be yer, then? Orf to see some gennelmun?"

Sarah knew her voice betrayed her origin and nodded. "For my lady," she whispered. "Please help me and I will pay you a shilling."

The promise of such largess, which he had only suggested as a joke between them, cheered the lad immediately. He turned around and set off up the street, and Sarah had to break into a run to keep up with him. After what seemed a long walk in the ill-fitting shoes that were far too large for her small feet and beginning to rub uncomfortably, they reached the broader thoroughfare of Piccadilly. The lad knew his way about and dodged nimbly past carriages and horses, only looking back now and then to check she was following him.

When they reached a stand for carriages he went boldly up to the driver and began to haggle in a low voice. As she felt for the shilling she had promised him she noticed a coin changing hands between her escort and the driver. Still, when the lad had disappeared with his money she climbed into the carriage gratefully, glad he had chosen an elderly decent-looking man who was kindly-disposed toward her. He at once assumed a fatherly air, concerned that she should be wandering abroad at this hour alone.

"I'll 'ave ye to Knightsbridge before ye can lick the

cat's ear," he promised genially. He closed the carriage door for her and moved off to climb laboriously into the driving seat.

The hackney smelt musty and damp and the seats were hard and not very clean. Sarah was so relieved to be on her way to a refuge with old Nanny that she would have happily traveled in far worse conditions if it meant she would soon be safe.

Not wishing to disclose her business to the driver, Sarah insisted on paying him his fare and seeing him drive off before she knocked on the door of the little cottage in the village of Knightsbridge. The place was in darkness on their arrival, and Sarah's heart sank at the thought of waking the inmates at such an hour to explain her predicament, but she had no choice. The driver seemed reluctant to leave her, but on being presented with a crown piece decided it was not his affair to argue with a young person, nor could he expect to understand the ways of ladies pretending to be servants. He drove off scratching his ear reflectively, intending to tell young Jeb to watch out in future whom he befriended, for a careful man never meddled with the gentry, whose wrath could be awful.

Sarah, left alone in the quiet high street, looked about her in some trepidation. The house was dark and shuttered, and for a dreadful moment she wondered if there was anyone at home at all. Her first timid knock produced no response, and when she banged harder on the brightly polished brass knocker there was still no sound from within. The neat garden offered no shelter and only a stray cat wandered up to yowl by her feet, hoping no doubt she would let him into the warmth of the house.

Desperately Sarah lifted the knocker and banged again and again. Someone must hear her. She was certain that Nanny would be there, for the old woman was retiring to live in this village and had mentioned no sudden move being planned by her sister. If she knocked repeatedly, someone must surely come.

A window screeched open above her, and a head poked out covered with a frilly nightcap. "Who is banging away at my door at midnight?" a voice yelled indignantly. "Be off with you now or I'll call the Watch," and before Sarah could answer the window banged down again.

"Please let me in," she called loudly. "I need shelter. Please open up the door." There was no response, and knowing that at least someone was inside, Sarah picked up the knocker and thumped it again with renewed vigor.

The window opened and a pail of slops was flung out, which narrowly missed the girl, though the foul smell reached her, as was intended. "Take that and go away," the voice shouted crossly. "Disturbing of a body in the night. Well, I never did!"

"Mrs. Pemberton. I've come to see Mrs. Pemberton," Sarah shouted as she heard the window being closed again.

There was a sudden silence and she could see two hands resting on the sill.

"I am Miss Davenant and I have come to seek shelter with Mrs. Pemberton, my old Nanny," she cried again, her voice almost breaking on a sob of desperation. "Please let me in to explain."

The window opened again cautiously above her and the face looked out. "Well, bless me," the voice said. "You don't look like Janet's Miss Sarah, that you don't."

"I am dressed in my maid's clothes. Please let me come in and talk to you," Sarah said. "It's so cold out here."

This apparently sounded right to the inmate of the bedroom, for a more friendly mutter reached her as the window closed and a light went on. She saw the flickering glow as a candle was carried down the stairs, and in a few moments the door opened and she was ushered inside. Mary, for it was Nanny's sister herself, pottered about lighting more candles and stoking the fire in the little hall which served as the living room of the cottage.

"Come you and sit down, miss," Mary murmured as the light now revealed the attractive features she recognized under the dirty shawl and cap. "Get you by the fire and then you can talk. I'll warm some milk for you too."

The stairs in the corner creaked, and Sarah looked around to see Nanny coming slowly down dressed in a long nightrobe with an old wrapper around her, her candle carried in one hand while with the other she steadied herself against the wall. Sarah flung herself on the old woman as she reached the bottom of the stairs, and all the pent-up emotion of the past few hours caused her to break into sobs.

"Hush, now, my little love. Nanny's here," she soothed as if Sarah were still a baby. "Come and tell me all about it now. You're safe here with us."

Feeling better in such reassuring surroundings, Sarah soon stopped crying and found the warm milk very soothing after her hectic evening. She told the two elderly women just what had happened and described the whole sorry mess without leaving out any detail. When she had finished, Nanny shook her head and the frills on her nightcap bobbed wildly. "I always said Master Dominic would go too far one day!" she exclaimed. "But to bandy his sister around as one would a sovereign—why, it's past all bearing! He is a naughty boy, and so I shall tell him when I see him again!"

This forthright approach caused Sarah to smile for the first time in hours, although she knew Nanny could not cure this particular problem with a scolding as she had dealt with their childish complaints. "He wants me to marry this man and will not help me, so I had to come to you," she explained. She stretched out her feet, now free of the cumbersome shoes, and wriggled her toes in the warmth from the fire.

"Quite right too," Nanny agreed. "You can stay with Mary and me as long as you please. Are you sure you have no wish to marry this fine gentleman and become a great lady, though?" she inquired gently. She had noticed a certain reticence about her charge when the girl had described the marquess and knew her feelings were more deeply involved than she had said.

"I don't know him," Sarah replied. "I only met him for the first time today, and not in the best of circumstances," she added, remembering how rudely she had flounced away that morning.

Now Nanny was sure her former charge was not as indifferent as she appeared to be, for this was a poor excuse. Maybe Master Dominic had known what he was doing when he made the bet or perhaps had even discussed the plan beforehand with this marquess as an unusual way to give his sister's hand in marriage. Nanny was never surprised at the odd capers the gentlemen got up to, particularly those who were rich enough to indulge themselves. However, if Sarah needed more time to compose herself and this marquess really wanted to marry her, no doubt he would follow up such a strange proposal and court the girl in the established manner. She hinted as much to Sarah, who promptly became flushed and angry.

"No. You don't understand at all, Nanny! You think because he is rich I must want to marry him, which is not true. Anyway, Dominic told me that he hoped to marry another girl, Miss Masterson, and had no real wish to marry me at all. He is forced to do so because of his honour." She spat the word out bitterly.

Nanny nodded her head. Her Miss Sarah liked the gentleman, at any rate, for otherwise she would not be jealous. Mary diverted all three of them by entering the conversation at this point. "Miss Masterson is said

64

to be the greatest beauty ever to be seen in London," she said, proud of her knowledge. "She has golden hair and looks wonderful on horseback, they say."

"Miss Sarah is very pretty, and none can ride like she can," Nanny put in placidly.

Sarah sniffed in disgust. How could mere prettiness compare with an accredited beauty? She sighed and stood up. "So now perhaps you will see why I have come away. The story will soon be forgotten and the marquess can marry this beauty as he wanted to. It will all work out very well." She looked as if this thought gave her no pleasure.

"But what about you and Master Dominic?" Nanny was always practical. "Now Lady Marchmont is dead, you have nowhere to go and must accept your half brother's charity unless you do decide to marry this gentleman. It would solve all your problems," she coaxed gently.

Sarah stamped her foot on the flagstones. "It might solve some but would create others," she insisted stormily. "And I won't be tossed about like a bundle of rubbish. Don't you want to shelter me?"

"Of course we do. You will always be welcome with Nanny."

"I can hear a coach coming along the road," Mary said, interrupting them. "I wonder who else is driving through Knightsbridge at this hour?"

Sarah paused at the foot of the stairs, and her heart began to thump wildly. Surely he had not followed her here? She had been positive Dominic would have forgotten all about Nanny, and he did not know where the old lady lived anyway. It must be some other traveler out late and using this road. But as the carriage stopped and she heard the horses stamping outside she knew this was not so. Muffled voices reached them, and Mary had already tweaked the curtain aside to peer out into the darkness.

"My, it's a fine carriage out there!" she exclaimed as a knock was heard at the door.

Sarah stayed where she was but shrank back against the wooden newel post, and Mary opened the door with trembling hands. " 'Tis a girl outside," she cried, "and quite safe."

Annie rushed in as soon as the door was unbarred, and Sarah relaxed. "Annie! Why did you come after me?" she cried out.

The words had hardly been uttered before she knew the reason why. The marquess stood framed in the doorway behind the maid, and his gaze was dark and unfathomable.

Mary fluttered around, but Nanny stood her ground in the center of the room. "Who are you?" she asked firmly, although she had already guessed. "Why do you come bothering us in the middle of the night?"

He bowed courteously. "I am the Marquess of Hawkeworth. I have come to find Miss Sarah Davenant, for she is late for her wedding," he said suavely. His glance raked over her grubby clothes and rested briefly on her bare feet before passing on to the shoes still left by the fireplace. "The chaplain awaits us, and your maid has brought the finery," he added.

"I am not coming," Sarah said defiantly. "Where is my brother?"

"He sped off to Lewes certain you had gone to seek shelter with your half brother," the marquess replied. "I was unable to stop him from his headlong rush," he added regretfully. Sarah saw that his eyes were now gleaming wickedly and knew he had arranged it all.

"He was always an impetuous boy," Nanny put in. "Do close the door, Mary, before we all catch cold. Will you take some refreshment before you go?" she added, as if this were a normal social call.

The marquess inclined his head. "I thank you, but no. We really should be on our way as soon as possible. But another time." His smile was full of charm and

Sarah saw her old nurse thaw visibly. She would have little help there, for the Marquess of Hawkeworth was the very epitome of all that Nanny considered a proper gentleman should be. His manners were impeccable—when he wanted them to be, she thought—and his dress quietly elegant and very expensive.

Sarah moved across to Annie, who stood between her and the marquess looking apprehensive. "Did you tell him about Nanny?" Sarah hissed softly.

"No, miss. 'Twas Edward did that," the girl said with a gulp of fright. "I would have told Master Dominic if I'd thought of it."

"Would you? Well, you can help me escape from the coach or you will leave my employ at once," Sarah muttered, keeping one eye on the marquess, who was explaining his plans to the two sisters with obvious success. "Next time when I disappear it will be where no one can find me. You must leave this cottage ahead of us and tell Edward to stop the coach at a spot where several roads meet. I can slip away unnoticed if you scream that we are to be attacked. But if you fail me . . ." She deliberately left the threat hanging between them.

Annie looked miserable and frightened, but as Sarah said goodbye to the two elderly women she was glad to see the maid had slipped out of the door, leaving it just ajar. She dared not contemplate what would happen if Annie failed her this time.

The girl was tucked into a corner of the coach when the marquess escorted Sarah to a seat beside her and sat down opposite himself.

"You were extremely quiet and biddable just now," he remarked conversationally. "I hope you are not planning another escape from me, for it will not work."

The smothered gasp from Annie's corner which Sarah heard infuriated her. The girl would give her away and the devil opposite would guess something was afoot. Apparently he did, for at her haughty disclaimer he reached across and lifted her chin so that her eyes met his.

"Don't try to run away," he said quietly. "I have no intention of harming you, but if you continue to thwart me you will regret it." The voice was steely. "London can be a cruel city for a young lady alone with no protector. You will do much better to stay with me."

"Maybe I don't think so," she rejoined fierily. "I have no wish to be mistress of any man by force."

"Nor will you be that I know of," he replied calmly, ignoring the insult. "I have told you we are on our way to our wedding."

"You cannot marry a woman who is unwilling," she flashed back at him. "No clergyman would dream of performing the marriage ceremony if the bride is dragged to the altar."

He regarded her strangely for a moment, and she found this disturbing. "I have thought of that. The clergyman I know of will be quite willing whatever the circumstances," he said finally. "However much you scream and object. So I advise you to accept me quietly and retain your dignity."

This advice was given in such a formal tone that Sarah was chilled. The man was inhuman. "I would prefer to wait and get married when my brother can give me away," she said in a small voice, hoping she might delay the ceremony if nothing else. A great deal could happen even in a few hours.

It seemed he divined her purpose, for he laughed softly. "Oh no. I have safely disposed of your brother to avoid any last-minute qualms of conscience on his part, so you need not appeal to me on that score. Nor is it any use your hoping dear Edward will oblige you by stopping so that you can attempt to run away again."

Her gasp mingled with Annie's at his exact knowledge of her plans. The man was fiendish. Sarah sat back in the seat and gave way to despair. It seemed she had no choice but to marry him if that was what he intended. Or was he taking her to some strange place to go through a sham ceremony? Would she lose her virtue and still be a single girl by the morning? The prospect was too awful to think about, but she shivered in spite of the warm rug the marquess had wrapped around her knees. Suddenly it seemed as if this night would never end.

Chapter 8

The journey seemed to be accomplished in a remarkably short time. Sarah found her thoughts whirling so much she could think of no successful plan to extricate herself from whatever the marquess had planned for her. When the coach drew to a halt she thought for one wild moment that Edward intended to help her after all, but Annie choked as Hawkeworth's gaze fell on her and only mumbled about changing cloaks with her mistress. She neither screamed nor attracted his attention, and even as Sarah moved quickly toward the far door away from him he reached out and clasped her wrist.

"Don't try it," he advised gently. "We have reached the chapel where the wedding will take place. You can cover your old clothes with your own cloak that your maid has brought. I'm afraid there is no time or place for you to put on one of your own dresses. You will have to do without the finery so beloved of the female race at such a time," he added dryly, releasing his hold on her.

Sarah rubbed her wrist automatically where his fingers had dug into her flesh. "I am not interested in my clothes," she murmured dully. "What I am wearing is the least of my problems."

As he moved past her to get out of the coach she saw him smile at this. "You are certainly different from any other ladies I know," he remarked, jumping to the ground. He remained by the door, preventing her escape, and conferred briefly with Edward, who then disappeared inside the building Sarah could just see behind them.

"Miss Sarah, here is the cloak," Annie whispered in a scared little voice, handing over the thick silken garment.

Grateful to be able to discard the rough woolen cloak she had been wearing, Sarah put on her own silk one and tossed aside her cotton cap. When she climbed out of the coach the marquess thought how lovely she looked in the flickering light of the lanterns outside the chapel. Her hair was disordered and her face still smudged with dirt, but she affected him more than any society beauty he had ever met.

Instinctively he took her hand in his. "Trust me," he murmured. "I mean you no harm."

Just for a moment Sarah believed him and felt reassured by his presence.

Then the illusion was spoiled. "And now for our wedding," he said in a different tone, as if regretting his own moment of weakness.

"Here?" Sarah queried in horror. She looked around but could see little in the darkness. The chapel was situated on a corner and lit by two lanterns outside the small doorway. The grounds of some large mansion loomed across the road, and the whole area was deserted, not even the Watch in sight for her to appeal to. "We cannot be married in that house!" she exclaimed. "This must be a place where you intend to ravish me, not marry me." She tried to pull away from him, but he took a firmer grip on her arm.

"Stop being stupid and think sensibly," he rapped out. "If you had done so earlier you could have been married by my brother-in-law's own chaplain in my

71

house. We could have been comfortable then instead of forced to come to this dreary hole. There is a chapel in this house run by a Dr. Keith and an assistant. He performs marriages for those who wish for a hasty ceremony or who are running away from a more suitable alliance, which is why I've come. This is the Mayfair Chapel."

"I see," she whispered, beginning to understand.

"I thought you might," he muttered, sounding grim once more. "For sufficient financial inducement the man would probably marry a pair of apes, but he will serve us well enough. If you dislike your surroundings you have only yourself to blame, which also applies to the absence of your brother. You have shown me I cannot trust you, but believe me, girl, I intend to marry you, not to ravish you. I wish you would put such silly notions out of your head. I prefer a willing woman." With this sharp rejoinder he took her forward as Edward came out of the doorway to meet them.

Sarah allowed herself to be led into the house and tried to still the thumping of her heart. She had heard of the notorious Mayfair Chapel, for who had not? Clandestine marriages were celebrated here daily, and a few months before the beautiful Miss Elisabeth Gunning had wed the Duke of Hamilton in this very place. No wonder the Marquess of Hawkeworth had no qualms about bringing her here. She could understand now why he had said the parson would marry them whatever her objections and even if she kicked and screamed. He was probably being heavily bribed, and there was nothing she could do now but go through with the ceremony.

The whole service was very brief. The parson, Dr. Keith, looked as if he had been hauled out of his bed to officiate, and he reeked of spirits. He gabbled the words that bound them together and clearly desired to return to his interrupted slumbers as soon as possible. Edward passed the marquess a ring, and Sarah allowed him to place it on her finger. Behind her she could hear Annie shuffling her feet in her eagerness to see all that went on, but Sarah only noticed that the young assistant had a running nose and a sore on his lip. The entire service seemed just a jumble of words to her, and she said what she was told and moved as if in a dream.

It was over before she was aware of it and they were back in the coach and moving off once more. "My house is not far away in Grosvenor Square," the marquess said politely. "I have ordered a room prepared for you, and I think you will find everything you need. My servants will bring you anything you wish."

Sarah nodded dumbly, but her voice had deserted her. She could find nothing to say and longed to get into bed and sleep. Maybe she would wake up and find this was all some terrible nightmare.

The marquess offered her his hand to assist her from the coach and led her into his imposing house himself. Annie still followed behind, looking about her at the sumptuous furnishings with awe. In the large marble-tiled entrance hall the marquess relinquished her hand.

"I will leave you in the capable hands of my house-keeper and your own maid," he said formally. "I will not see you again until tomorrow morning," he added pointedly, "when we will discuss settlements." He bowed and moved away, disappearing into a book-lined room at the back of the hall.

For a moment Sarah wanted to call out to him to stay with her and not to leave her in such strange surroundings, but she resisted the temptation. She must be weak with tiredness even to have contemplated such a thing, she decided, as she allowed herself to be undressed and put to bed in the luxurious room shown her by Mrs. Robins, the housekeeper. Annie attended to her and wisely said little about what had happened. She remembered her mistress's threat to dismiss her but hoped that Miss Sarah herself would forget all about it now she was safely married. The mistress was lucky, Annie

73

thought, to wed such a fine gentleman as the marquess, and she would realize it soon enough when she got used to her new position. The maid tiptoed away, and Sarah slept almost at once in spite of her troubled thoughts and fears for the future.

She awoke late next morning and sat up expecting to find herself in her chamber at the Thatched House Tavern. Instead she saw the pale-blue silk hangings picked out in gold around the bed and the elegant gilt furniture in the room and realized her mistake. The night's adventure came back to her with startling clarity, and she looked down at her hand in fright. A large sapphire-and-diamond ring showed her that her new status as wife was real and not a figment of her imagination. She was still staring at it in fascination when Annie knocked and entered, carrying a tray of hot chocolate and warm bread rolls. She plumped up the pillows and placed the tray beside the bed, then paused to admire the ring.

"It's beautiful, Miss Sarah—or should I say Mistress now?" She giggled nervously.

"My lady," Sarah told her coldly, remembering how the girl she had trusted had let her down. "What did the marquess pay you and Edward to betray me?"

Annie started and flushed an unbecoming red. She clasped her hands together and looked more frightened than ever, reminding Sarah of a trapped rabbit. "Nothing, miss—I mean, my lady. At least he gave me nothing, but I think he promised Edward he would see us provided for. He promised us a house," she added eagerly, and then stopped in dismay, realizing what she had said.

"I see." Sarah did only too well. "You have no loyalty at all, Annie, so you may leave me."

"Leave you? But I am still to serve you, my lady. The marquess said so," the girl blurted out, beginning to twist her apron between her hands.

"But I may not want a maid who will not have her

74

mistress's interests at heart," Sarah snapped back. "How could you join my enemies?" She thrust herself out of bed and crossed the room to look out of the window.

Behind her Annie began to sob. " 'Twasn't my fault you was gambled over. I did nothing, but Edward said 'twould be the best for us and for you to go along with this lord. I only did what I thought was for the best," she sniffed, her country accent coming out strongly in her distress.

Sarah turned round and saw the girl's misery. She ran across the room and hugged her impulsively. "I'm sorry, Annie. I have been very unkind to you, but I was so upset. I didn't want to marry this man, and now I have I don't know what I shall do," she added bleakly. Her arms dropped to her sides again. "I would rather keep you as my maid, for then I will have one friendly face that I know near me."

"Oh, Miss Sarah—my lady—it will not be so bad when you get used to it," Annie said optimistically. "He is a handsome man and has such manners. You will grow to like him before long, you see if you don't." She had recovered herself now and began to lay out clothes. "His lordship has had your bags sent around from the Thatched House Tavern, and Master Dominic's," she added.

This sign of his efficiency did not surprise his new bride. He was a man who knew what he wanted and always obtained it, if his dealings with her were any-thing to go on. She wished Annie had not said that about liking him, for she knew the maid was right. She already did find him very attractive and could imagine that marriage to him would be all she desired if he had only felt the same way. But she knew he loved another and wanted to marry her and would probably have done so but for Dominic's stupid bet. She sighed. He had seemed so concerned about her just before they went into that chapel, and then he had changed again and become the cold man she had seen before. What had he said? He had told her not to be stupid because she imagined he wanted to ravish her, and now that assumption of hers made her blush with shame. How could such a man as the Marquess of Hawkeworth find her attractive when he could pick and choose among the beauties of London and was said to be a courtier of the reigning toast? Mary's words describing the fair Miss Masterson made Sarah set her mouth in determined lines. Very well. They had been forced into marrying, but if he did not want her then she would be unattainable also. No man like the marquess was going to imagine she was languishing after him. Maybe Annie, Edward, and Nanny were right, and even Dominic. She would be in a very fine position now, and she would make the most of it. If he allowed her plenty of money then she would spend it and he could regret marrying her for all she cared.

Thus it was that an hour later when Sarah, dressed in her most handsome morning gown of palest-green twilled silk, came downstairs she had put aside her fears and hidden her weakness. The marquess had just finished breakfast and was strolling out of the dining room as she reached the hall. He bowed over her hand and complimented her on her appearance.

"Your new servant, my maid, Annie, knows how to do her job," Sarah replied sweetly. "You have an acquisition in her and Edward. Dominic, my brother, always found Edward an excellent groom, but he can turn his hand to anything."

Accepting this challenge without a blink, the marquess nodded. "I thought they deserved a more stable household to work in, with their talents," he agreed smoothly and watched her flash him a glance of fury. "Now if we could stop this exchange of insults before you get heated, I have something to discuss with you."

Sarah was immediately annoyed at his calm assumption she would be the one to grow angry. She nodded her head and followed him down the hall, determined not to give him that pleasure, whatever he said to her. He flung open the door of the room he had retired to the night before, and she preceded him inside.

"This is my favorite retreat," Hawkeworth admitted with a disarming smile that transformed his face and made her heart leap. "When I'm tired or in low spirits I come in here and try to forget the world outside." He was surprised at himself for telling her this and betraying a part of himself he normally kept well hidden.

"It's a beautiful room!" Sarah exclaimed, moving forward eagerly. "My father's library was always his favorite room, and mine too, although Dominic preferred the gun room. Papa was a scholar, you know, but he allowed me to trespass into his sanctum and read his books whenever I wished." She moved toward the laden bookshelves down one side of the room and scanned the titles, murmuring to herself when she recognized one. The Marquess let her do so and sat himself down in a deep leather armchair beside the fire, which was burning brightly to ward off the April chill.

Sarah left the books reluctantly and came back to stand beside another chair. She admired the polished wooden table in the window and thought how much more attractive it would be with a bowl of spring flowers on it to catch the reflections and bring color to the browns and dull reds elsewhere. "What did you wish to say?" she asked politely.

"Sit down first, and then I will tell you," he said peremptorily, but added, "You make me feel uncomfortable. No gentleman should sit while a lady stands, and I like to relax in this chair." Again he smiled, and Sarah responded by smiling back at him and sinking down into the seat opposite.

He did not speak at once but gazed into the fire for a moment. "I think if you stop to consider it you can understand my motives for marrying you quickly," he began. "I want it to appear to the fashionable world that we could not wait for a conventional courtship and so decided to wed immediately. By this I hope that all gossip attached to your brother's unfortunate bet and my acceptance of it may be seen in the light of a romantic joke since we were secretly betrothed anyway." He looked at her somberly, guessing from her flushed cheeks and agitated manner that she was about to object strongly. "Don't say anything until I've finished," he advised. "This is all such a muddle that we must attempt to make the best of it, both of us, and I believe this to be the most sensible way of doing so. I have to admit I had no intention of marrying just yet, but my relatives will be delighted." He looked rueful.

Sarah's happy mood had gone with his words, which brought back her miserable situation. "What you are suggesting is that we present to the world the picture of a romantic attachment and a marriage due to mutual affection and esteem which is far from the case," she snapped.

He raised his eyebrows, but nodded. "You have put it bluntly, but yes, that is what I want. If you can manage to carry off such a deception, then we should still the gossiping tongues which are always so ready to wag at every tidbit they can find."

"At all costs we must still the gossiping tongues," she agreed with honeyed sweetness. "How dreadful it would be if the slightest breath of scandal attached to the fair name of Hawkeworth!"

"Or to that of Davenant," he returned coolly. He stood up and moved away from her so that she could no longer see his face. "From your words I gather you will find this difficult. Don't be alarmed. I have married you to give you the benefit of my name and protection, certainly, but I will make no demands upon you at all. It will be a marriage in name only. As I think I have already said, I will have nothing to do with an unwill-

ing female. However, you will not find me ungenerous. I will make you an allowance, the first quarter to be paid at once. I will undertake to house your brother and support him. I might even find him some gainful occupation," he added sardonically. "You will not lose by becoming the Marchioness of Hawkeworth, I assure you. But in return I expect you to play your part in public, although you may see nothing of me in private. I have invited several members of my family to dine tonight to meet my new bride. I shall want you to act as my hostess, naturally. We will dine at five, but no doubt they will arrive by four at the latest."

He turned around, and once more she found his gaze unfathomable. "They will be anxious to see the woman who has managed to snare me at last. I hope you will not disappoint them. Your servant." He bowed low, and before she could think of something cutting to say, he had left the library and she was alone.

Chapter 9

The Marquess of Hawkeworth paced up and down the
gold salon on the first floor and waited for his family to
arrive. He was dressed formally in evening attire. His
breeches were palest-gray silk fastened at the knee
with a silver bow, and his heavy black ribbed silk coat
was cut in the newest fashion with shorter skirts,
while his silver-embroidered waistcoat set off the delicate Mechlin lace at his throat and cuffs. His wig was
dark and drawn back from his face into a queue fastened by a black silk bow. His only concessions to the
excesses of the moment were a light powdering of his
wig and a gold fob at his waist, while he carried an
enameled snuffbox and now and again took a pinch.

  He was deep in thought and frowning when the door
opened and a footman announced the arrival of his
brother-in-law James Turner, only thirty-eight and
already a bishop. His loving family had not been surprised at the honours bestowed upon this worthy, pompous man whose intellect was exceeded only by his high
opinion of himself. The marquess disliked him only a
little more than his oldest sister, who was married to
him and due to illness was unable to accompany him to
the family gathering. For this the marquess mentally

thanked heaven as he stifled a sigh and prepared to be bored as he moved forward to greet his guest.

With the civilities over, the bishop, who looked far older than his years, launched at once into the attack. "I gather you dispensed with my chaplain, Gerald," he said stiffly. "Was there a particular reason for dismissing him so abruptly, or did you feel I should have made myself available at such short notice?"

Hawkeworth groaned inwardly. This was going to be more difficult than he had anticipated, and he reluctantly decided he would have to put the blame onto his new wife if he hoped to get out of the situation. "I'm afraid my Sarah is incurably romantic, James," he explained with a slight smile. "She took this notion into her head to be married at the same chapel where the Duke and Duchess of Hamilton were wed. I could hardly gainsay her so early on," he added.

His brother-in-law looked at him in some disbelief. "You surprise me, Gerald, you really do! I have never known you to do anything you didn't want to, least of all for a woman. She must be an exceptional young lady, and I can hardly wait to be introduced. However, I must point out that your union is scarcely beginning in the most auspicious manner, since you were joined in holy wedlock by an unfrocked priest." He pursed his lips and looked as disapproving as such a portly man could. "I really feel you should have permitted my chaplain to perform the ceremony. I do hope that we are not expected to condone a hole-in-the-corner affair? She is not some flighty piece you would be ashamed to marry in church, I hope?" he asked suspiciously.

"Would I have asked you here so soon to meet her, James, if that were the case?" countered the marquess quickly. "I realize you must disapprove of my wedding's being conducted in the Mayfair Chapel, but I am counting on you to remedy the situation by giving us a formal blessing in your church to regularize the affair in the best possible way. I shall then have satisfied everyone. You will not fail me, will you?"

Before the bishop could frame an adequate reply, the marquess had moved forward to greet his mother and youngest sister, who was still unmarried. He was very fond of Lydia, counting her the best of his female relatives, and he usually gave her more of his attention than he bestowed on any other member of his family. She was only eighteen, the same age as his bride, he reflected, and he found it hard to satisfy her curiosity and to answer all her eager questions. His mother was disapproving and prepared to dislike the bride on sight, since the girl had married her only son without her consent or even her knowledge. She was justifiably incensed at the nature of the wedding and said so roundly.

"It is too shabby of you, Gerald, to upset me so," she mourned almost at once. "I have been longing to see you happily settled, but to a sensible girl of my choosing, and now you suddenly spring a marriage like this on us all. Who is she? I have never heard of her. Have I ever met her? Has she been presented at court?"

The marquess did his best to answer her and was grateful to see his sister Phoebe for almost the first time in his life. She was older than he was and resembled his brother-in-law James, being pompous, conceited, and very fat. She was dark, as were most of the Hawkeworths, but his mother's good looks had passed her by and he continually marveled at any man's being able to stand her long nose and disapproving stare while to bed with her—here his mind always refused to function any further. He greeted her politely enough, and her meek little spouse, Sir Arnold Frencham. He cleverly turned the attention of Phoebe to his mother, and both women were soon discussing the reason for the hasty marriage and wondering what could have possessed Gerald to act in a manner that was so uncharacteristic of him.

When Sarah made her entrance it was to find almost all her husband's relations already assembled. She stood poised in the doorway and surveyed them with an appraising stare that the marquess recognized as challenging but he hoped would pass unnoticed by the rest. He moved to her side, and so did Lydia, and she was the first to speak.

"Sarah? I may call you Sarah, may I not? I am so happy to meet you," Lydia said, clasping the girl's hand impulsively. "I have been wanting Gerry to marry for an age now, but none of the simpering misses in London have been nearly good enough for him. I can see that you are different, though. I am sure we shall become firm friends in no time."

Sarah returned the handclasp and found herself smiling in real pleasure. It was impossible not to respond to Lydia's engaging friendliness, and her welcome made up somewhat for the icy stares from the rest of the group gathered in the salon.

"Don't be scared of them," Lydia whispered in her ear as the marquess led his bride over to present her to his mother. "Phoebe is a prig, but James is not so bad, and at least my sister Susan isn't with him. Mama will soon get over her miff at this secret marriage if she finds you a biddable girl." She dimpled mischievously. "I myself think it is so romantic. Fancy being married in the Mayfair Chapel! I do envy you."

"Enough, Lydia. You cannot monopolize Sarah all the evening. Mama, may I present my new bride, the former Miss Sarah Davenant," the marquess said.

Curtsying low, Sarah tried not to object to the disapproving glare of the young woman in puce satin standing nearby, who she discovered was Phoebe. The marquess's mother, now the dowager Lady Hawkeworth, was still a handsome woman. She was dressed in dark-blue silk with diamonds at her throat and an elaborate powdered coiffure and looked a regal figure. Bearing in mind Lydia's comment about being biddable, Sarah allowed Lady Hawkeworth to make some disastrously pointed comments about hasty weddings, endured insinuations about her possible condition that might have necessitated this, and answered all the personal questions addressed to her as patiently and politely as she could. She found the sharp and acid comments of Lady Frencham almost too much to bear without some retort but managed to hold her tongue.

She was really grateful when the marquess came over and rescued her, tucking her arm into his possessively. She was so relieved she smiled at him with unusual warmth, and his mother was moved to say to her older daughter: "I really think he has found just the right girl. See how fondly they look at one another. It is all most irregular, but now I have spoken to her I remember her family well enough, and she will not disgrace us. She seems a quiet little thing."

"She's passably pretty, I suppose," Phoebe said grudgingly. "At least we will not have to endure that Masterson chit now. I was opposed to Gerald's marrying her. Reigning beauties are often so vulgar." She sniffed. She had been against her brother's marrying the season's catch, for she had no desire to be completely eclipsed by such a beauty, and since this bride was neither dark nor fair she considered her looks not worthy of notice.

James Turner was not interested in the appearance of his brother-in-law's wife but he was concerned in case she was ill-bred, or frivolous, better suited to mistress than wife. On being introduced he was pleasantly surprised, but after the lengthy dinner he managed to seat himself beside her and found her intellect surprising. He was so impressed by her conversation and her knowledge that his wife's elderly Aunt Jemima was forced to shoo him away with her fan in order to be able to enjoy her share of the evening's entertainment.

"Gerald is a luckier man than he knows," the old lady said cheerfully as she settled down for a comfortable gossip. "I knew your mother years ago, and she was a gal of spirit and accomplishment. You take after her from what I can see."

Sarah smiled. "I'm sure I am not nearly so pretty," she said demurely, casting her eyes down into her lap.

The old lady leaned across and tapped her with the handle of her ivory fan. "Nonsense, m'dear. Very sweetly said, but you are no simpering miss. You can't fool me, although you can probably hoodwink this crowd of ninnies. That stuffed ass James loves to have someone to lecture, and Phoebe disapproves of everyone anyway and you less than some. Tell me about this bet now," she added curiously. "Is it true my nephew won your hand at the card table?"

Sarah looked into a pair of very shrewd gray eyes in a lined and wrinkled face and decided not to lie to this formidable lady but to tell her at least part of the truth. "I have to admit that my brother and my husband did enjoy a game together for a joke and staked my person for the winner."

"Heard it said that you have been romantically attached to Gerald for some time and have been keeping it secret?" She cocked an eye at Sarah and waited expectantly for a reply.

"That is the story that is going around," Sarah agreed cautiously.

"Stuff!" said Aunt Jemima rudely. "You can't gammon me, gal. I have it for a fact your brother had never met my nephew before that night at the tables and nor had you."

Sarah felt herself blushing and tried vainly not to appear upset by this information.

"Don't worry. I have no intention of telling anyone else that particular tidbit," she cackled. "I don't know what Gerald has been up to, or you either, but I think you will be just right for him. Maybe he doesn't know that yet himself, but he will find out. Don't let him walk over you, gal. Give him as good as you get." She heaved herself out of her chair. "Now I intend to take myself off and that silly sister of mine. Deaf as a post and past seventy—she shouldn't be allowed out," the old lady said cheerfully. "Won't recognize you again either. Never mind. Remember what I said, child, and give him as good as you get."

With this she moved off to make her farewells, and Sarah was relieved to find the other members of the family doing the same. Lady Frencham was stiff and distant, but her husband smiled in a friendly way when his wife had passed on toward the door and patted her hand genially. Aunt Jemima and Aunt Matilda had already gone, but Sarah was invited to enjoy a nuncheon with her new mama-in-law the following day, and Lydia squealed happily.

"Oh, we can have a real chat afterward when Mama is resting," she promised. "I do hope Gerry will invite me to stay for a while to get to know you and enjoy myself. I could do with a change."

The marquess was at that moment, to his amazement, receiving the congratulations of Bishop Turner on his choice of a wife. "She has a very fine understanding for a lady," James said patronizingly. "Her knowledge of the classics is quite remarkable. She could teach you a thing or two of Latin and Greek," he added tactlessly. "Very pleasant manner, too, so I think we can overlook the irregularity of your union. I will be happy to give you a blessing. We can fix the date in the morning." He was the last to go and left the Marquess for once bereft of speech in the middle of the salon.

Feeling she had just survived an ordeal almost as bad as the one she had gone through the night before, Sarah sank down onto an elegant chaise longue and fanned herself gently.

"Was it that bad?" inquired the marquess.

She looked up and made a rueful face. "Oh, not meeting your mother and younger sister Lydia, no, of course not. But how do you make polite conversation with your Aunt Matilda, sir? She never heard a thing I said and seemed to imagine I was your mother's sister and not your bride. It is unfair of you to laugh, for I found it very disconcerting," she said with some spirit.

"I'm sure you did. Aunt Matty has been a trial to us all for years, but if it is any comfort I see her only once or twice in a twelvemonth if I'm forced to, so you can forget her for a long while. How did you manage with dear James?" he added curiously, for he had not yet got over his surprise at her success in that quarter.

"I found him a trifle stuffy," she admitted. "Still, he has quite a fair knowledge of Homer, I think, although he misquoted several passages, but we discussed Shakespeare and found ourselves in agreement over his sonnets."

"Did you indeed!" There was no concealing his amazement now. "Misquoted Homer, you say? James! I can't believe it. Did you tell him so?" he asked.

Her face broke into a smile, and he noticed suddenly she had a delightful dimple at one side of her mouth. "No. I'm afraid I couldn't pluck up the courage to do so," she admitted. "I feared your wrath if I upset him, so I contented myself with quoting some passages correctly."

The marquess sat down beside her, and his face showed his admiration. "I have married a bluestocking, I can see. No wonder James was congratulating me. I have never been known to keep company with ladies of intellect before." At once he cursed himself for a tactless fool. Her face grew solemn and her expression cold. He tried to make amends. "I think Lydia has taken a fancy to you too. She is already pressing me to invite her to stay with us so that you can take her around to all the balls and ridottos that my mother no longer feels up to. Don't worry—I will put her off somehow."

"I should like her to come," Sarah said impulsively. "It would be pleasant to have company of my own age,

87

and I should enjoy taking her about, for I have done little of that myself as yet. You would not object?"

"Not at all. So long as you don't encourage her in extravagance. I never knew such a girl for spending money as my little sister." He got to his feet again. "Even Phoebe had less acid comments to make than usual, and I'm certain she came determined to be unpleasant."

"I have not sufficient looks to upset her dignity," Sarah said with deceptive meekness.

"I beg your pardon!"

"That is what your sister said, or at least nearly so, according to Lydia. I am merely passing pretty and not likely to bring undue comment down on the Hawkeworth family," she quoted naughtily. "Nor did she believe the tales of betting or a romance, for a gentleman of your breeding would never lower himself to the one nor fall for the other."

"Did she say all that?" he exclaimed wrathfully. "By heavens, she is an impossible creature to be so rude about my bride in my own house!" He was clearly very annoyed, and Sarah found herself feeling rather pleased.

"Oh, she was not being rude, sir, but complimentary, so Lydia assured me," Sarah added.

He glanced down and noted the dimple once more. "I could wring her neck all the same," he remarked slightly more cheerfully. "How poor Arnold puts up with her I don't know. He has all my sympathy."

"And mine," Sarah agreed.

"You have endured my family with remarkable patience, and for that I thank you," he said, and he sounded genuinely grateful. "My mother believes the story I put about anyway and was graciously pleased to tell me she approves of you if not of the way we scrambled into matrimony. I think we may confound the gossipmongers and quell the rumors after all."

Sarah rose at once on hearing this. "It is to be hoped we manage to do that," she said sweetly. "Otherwise my play-acting this evening would have been in vain." She swept him a curtsy and turned on her heel, leaving the salon before he could think of something to say to convince her it was her welfare as much as his own that he was concerned about.

Chapter 10

The following day found Sarah driving north to Cavendish Square to visit Lady Hawkeworth in an unsettled state of mind. She had been delighted to win her new husband's approval and gratitude the evening before, but he had spoiled his compliments by referring to the wretched scandal they had suppressed, proving that his only interest was in his family name and nothing more. She had found their pretense of marital bliss very pleasant and could imagine enjoying her life if this were genuine on both sides. As it was, she knew she herself was in danger of finding him more and more irresistible while his own affections were clearly engaged elsewhere.

If she had hoped this to be merely a rumor, Lydia soon enlightened her to the real state of affairs that afternoon.

Nuncheon was taken in a small dining room on the first floor of Lady Hawkeworth's small but elegant mansion. The dowager was gracious but condescending to the new bride, though as the meal progressed she began to thaw and was soon treating Sarah in the same way as her own younger child, Lydia. That damsel had prevailed upon her mama to permit her to visit the newlyweds, although Lady Hawkeworth demurred slightly, wondering if this would be considered suitable in the circumstances.

"Why not, Mama?" Lydia pouted immediately as they sat down in the withdrawing room. "Gerry has invited me, and I can go and stay with him now because I will have a chaperon in Sarah, which was always your excuse for not permitting me to go before."

"Yes, I know that, dear," Lady Hawkeworth admitted with what seemed like a trace of embarrassment. She fanned herself energetically. "But your brother probably meant you to come in a few weeks' time, not right away."

"Oh, I'm sure he didn't," Lydia objected.

"Just think," her mama broke in quickly before the girl could go on. "Dear Gerald and Sarah have only just entered into marriage and might like time on their own for adjustment. Maybe they are even contemplating a prolonged wedding trip. I know my own dear Ernest took me to Paris for three months after our wedding." She sighed and fanned herself again, but with less enthusiasm.

Lydia looked sideways at Sarah. "Do you want to be left alone to bill and coo?" she demanded. "I never thought of Gerry as that type of man. Females have never seemed very important to him. I know he usually had his ladies on the side, so I don't know how he will feel now."

"Lydia!" Lady Hawkeworth was scandalized. "A well-brought-up young lady does not mention such matters and should know nothing of a gentleman's interests outside the home!"

Sarah knew something of the marquess's interests and would have preferred not to, but decided now was the time to intervene. "Lydia didn't mean anything, I'm sure," she said, smoothing over the awkward moment, for she could see the girl was upset at her own tactlessness. "I would be delighted to have Lydia's company straightaway, and I'm certain if her brother asked her himself he must have wanted her to come."

"Well, if you're sure," Lady Hawkeworth said doubtfully. "It does seem rather soon after the wedding to me." She sounded rather disappointed at Sarah's lack of romance.

"My husband did suggest we might make a trip in a few months' time instead of immediately so that I can get together a good wardrobe before going. I've been so long in Sussex I must be very dowdy," Sarah hastened to explain.

The dowager was mollified by this. She could understand any young lady's desire for a new wardrobe of clothes in the very latest fashion, and although she admired her new daughter-in-law's taste, now she thought about it perhaps her dresses were slightly out of the current mode. So she nodded happily. "Then Lydia can certainly accompany you. I am glad to hear you will take a trip later. Gerald could do with a change, and if he takes you to Paris you could always buy finer clothes there."

Before her mother-in-law could suggest an immediate trip to the French capital, Sarah began a discussion of what Lydia should bring with her and had no difficulty in diverting both ladies from the former subject. However, Lady Hawkeworth was soon exhausted and professed herself ready to lie down for a short while. She took her leave of them both after giving Lydia a wealth of good advice which that young lady accepted but promptly told Sarah she would ignore when the door closed behind her mother.

The rest of the afternoon passed in a whirl of preparations for Lydia's forthcoming stay. Sarah was amazed at the amount of luggage her new relative considered necessary to take with her and felt quite sorry for her harassed maid who had such a mountain of packing to do.

Finally they were settled in the marquess's chaise

and bowling back to Grosvenor Square. It was at this moment that Lydia tucked her arm through Sarah's and said confidentially: "I'm so glad you married my brother instead of Delia Masterson. We all thought he intended to propose to her, so you can imagine our surprise when we were invited to meet his bride yesterday. I thought you might be fair, as she is, but I'm glad you are not. I think fair hair insipid myself," she added, tossing her own dark curls. "And prettiness is not everything. You are much more fun."

Knowing she was being paid a compliment of a sort, Sarah tried hard not to mind her lack of beauty in the eyes of the Hawkeworth family, whose standards were clearly very high. She would also have to grow resigned to references connecting the marquess and the beautiful Miss Masterson.

Lydia chatted on, describing her brother's former interest in the beauty, unaware that her listener did not really want to hear all that she said. "Delia has been favoring Gerry and Lord Marchmont about equally, although I don't think anyone could prefer that skinny overdressed creature to my brother, do you?"

"I have never met Lord Marchmont," Sarah admitted, "so I cannot compare them."

"Well, take it from me he is overbearing, and only a few months ago nobody had heard of him. He inherited his aunt's wealth and the title; he was a nephew or cousin or something," Lydia explained vaguely. "But Delia would have married Gerry in the end, for she wanted his money and his title. Lord Marchmont is rich, but not as rich as Gerry is, so she would never have chosen him. I think now that Gerry must have been courting her just for fun to spite Marchmont, since he has married you, and in such a romantic way. Do tell me all about your wedding. I do so want to know just what it was like at the Mayfair Chapel, and I couldn't ask you in front of Mama because she would not have approved." Lydia giggled.

In some relief Sarah saw they had reached the Hawkeworth house in Grosvenor Square, and the coach was drawing up. Before she could reply the footman had let down the steps and was helping her to alight.

"You must tell me later," Lydia insisted as she followed.

No sooner had they been ushered into the hall by the butler than they heard the sound of raised voices coming from the small salon to the right of the front entrance. The door was open, and it was impossible not to hear what was said.

"I tell you I must see Lord Hawkeworth immediately. My sister has disappeared, and he is responsible. When I find him I shall call him out," echoed around them.

Lydia looked startled, and her eyes gleamed with interest. Sarah, recognizing Dominic's voice, started forward.

"His lordship will return within the hour, if you would wait here," said another voice, which Sarah guessed belonged to one of the servants.

"I want to see him now," Dominic burst out.

"Hold on, Davenant. Don't get hasty," said another man.

"Oh, that is Peter," squealed Lydia and rushed past Sarah into the room.

It was Sir Peter Trevenning trying to restrain her brother, Sarah noticed, as she followed quickly behind. The harassed secretary employed by the marquess was beginning to explain again that his master would return shortly when Dominic caught sight of her.

"Sarah!" he exclaimed. "What are you doing here? I thought you had gone to Sussex, but Thomas hadn't seen you. We searched around and then when I got back to town your traps had all been taken from the Thatched House. What are you doing here?"

"I'll explain everything in a moment, Dominic. Do please be quiet," Sarah said desperately. She had seen

Lydia's interest in his words and feared he might make a rash statement and let their secret out. "Mr. Clarke, you can leave the visitors with me," she added for the secretary's benefit and saw him slip out of the room in relief as Dominic began again.

"Look here, Sarah, what have you been doing? Why did you disappear anyway if you meant to get in touch with the man later? Why, you could have been married by now and everything hushed up sensibly."

"I am married," Sarah said clearly, and at once there was silence.

Lydia was hanging onto Sir Peter's arm and looking from one to the other of them while the marquess's friend watched the scene through half-closed eyes.

"Married?" Dominic shouted, stopping in midstride toward her. "Married, you say?"

"Yes. Married to the Marquess of Hawkeworth, as you wished," Sarah said more quietly. "You know we wanted it all to be kept a secret and only the two of us to be present, so we waited until you had gone to Sussex and then slipped away to the wedding." She hoped desperately he would accept this and not ask any awkward questions while Lydia was in the room. "May I introduce my new sister-in-law, Lydia," she added quickly to forestall him.

Remembering his manners, Dominic swung around and made a swift bow. As he acknowledged her greeting he also became aware of her charming features and the dark curls bobbing round her face. He could not fail to notice her interest in the conversation either and made a heroic effort to control his anger and curiosity.

"My congratulations, Lady Hawkeworth," Sir Peter put in, making a sweeping leg. "I can understand why Gerald wished to keep you away from his friends, for such loveliness would soon be stolen from him otherwise."

Sarah acknowledged the compliment and felt relieved at his tact in bridging the awkward gap. She recognized him as the man who had accompanied the marquess on that first morning and thought he probably knew the real truth of the affair.

"Do you know Sarah?" Lydia asked him eagerly. "We have only just met, really, but already we are friends and I am coming to spend some weeks here with her and Gerry."

"Are you indeed?" drawled her brother from the doorway. "I wonder Mama permitted you to come."

"Oh, hallo, Gerry. Sarah persuaded Mama that she wanted me and so I'm here. You will let me stay, won't you?" Lydia added rather anxiously, remembering her mother's words about newly wedded couples.

"If Sarah wants you, then of course you must stay," the marquess replied enigmatically as he strolled in.

"My brother has arrived back from Sussex," Sarah said with a rush.

"So I see. Welcome to my house, Dominic. I hope you can stay with us for a long while," the marquess said courteously, completely surprising that young man and leaving him speechless. "Peter, how nice to see you," Hawkeworth added, turning to his old friend. "Have you also returned from foreign parts?" His dark eyebrows rose in a mocking way.

"From the country, yes. Unfortunately my errand was fruitless, as you possibly know," Sir Peter said blandly. "But I am sure I will be rewarded for my efforts on behalf of friendship."

"Of course. I expect you to dine with us. Now, Lydia, run along and get settled in. I'm sure Mrs. Robins has given you your old room. You will want to unpack."

"I would rather stay and find out just what you are all talking about. You are keeping something from me," she retorted cheekily.

"Run along, Lydia, or I will send you back to Mama," the marquess said firmly. He took her arm and propelled her to the door. "Our other guests are also about to. retire to dress for dinner, and I might just wish to be alone with my wife, you know."

"Oh. Yes, I see," Lydia agreed in sudden understanding. "I never thought of that."

The marquess closed the door firmly on her retreating figure and sighed. "I hope you haven't done anything rash," he said to Dominic. "I had your bags moved with your sister's to my house, and you will find them in a suite which has been prepared for you."

"Here?"

"Don't sound so horrified. I'm sure you have been told I am now your brother-in-law, so we will have to get used to one another. And forget all that about that disastrous bet and the subsequent furor," he added meaningly.

Dominic eyed him with respect tempered by awe. "When I have heard just what happened to Sarah," he agreed. "From her own lips," he added just as pointedly.

The marquess yawned to show he was bored with the subject. "I'm sure she will gratify your curiosity in due course. Now I suggest you dress for dinner, or you will never remove the marks of travel in time."

Dominic looked as if he was about to object, but Sarah took his arm and nodded. "I will see you later," she promised.

"Are you all right?" he said anxiously. "You look well, but how long have you been here? When did you marry?"

"I was married that same night in the Mayfair Chapel and have been here ever since," she told him. "Now go and dress. We can talk later."

He moved reluctantly toward the hall. "I wish I understood all that has been going on," he said plaintively. "I never thought you would deceive me, but you must have done if you married him that same night. I would have liked to be at your wedding to be sure you were happy."

"I know. I would have liked you to be," she murmured.

97

"Later, Dominic," the marquess said forcefully from behind them. "All explanations will wait until after the dinner hour. I'm sure you must be famished if you have just driven up from Sussex." His tone was inexorable and allowed of no discussion. Dominic took the hint and left the room, and a footman escorted him to the apartments prepared for him.

With another bow to Sarah, Sir Peter also left the room to change his own linens in a guest chamber, and she was alone with her husband.

"I trust you enjoyed your day?" he inquired politely.

"Oh yes. Your mother was very kind and has almost forgiven me for being unknown to her before our marriage."

He smiled, and she was aware of the depths of his charm. "In time I'm sure she will grow as fond of you as she is of her own daughters. She was merely irritated at not being the one to introduce us, that's all."

"No one introduced us," she reminded him.

"If I recollect, you walked straight into me. I'm not sure if I should take it as a compliment or a direct insult that you could have been so oblivious of a man in my position."

"I never noticed you," Sarah admitted, frowning slightly as she thought back to her behavior.

"Ah! As I thought, it was an insult. I am truly humbled!"

"That would be impossible," she declared roundly. "And I would rather you did not refer to that morning."

"But I like spitting kittens," he teased her, enjoying her discomfiture and the way her eyes sparkled and her cheeks grew rosy.

Not certain how to take him in this mood, which was different from any she had seen in him so far, Sarah retreated into her dignity. "I beg you to excuse me, sir. If we are to dine at five o'clock I must go and change."

He reached out and took hold of her wrist as she rose from her curtsy. "You don't need to be so formal with me, and I hope you will not always run away when we are left alone," he said gently.

Afraid of betraying her desire to remain with him, Sarah resorted to coolness. "Why should I stay?" she asked, tossing her curls. "You said this was to be a marriage of convenience and I need not see you in private."

He released her wrist at once and bowed formally. "So I did, madam, so I did. Permit me to open the door for you. I have no wish to keep you waiting."

Sarah ran up the stairs to her room with a sinking heart, knowing she had offended him beyond reason and furious at her own stupidity. Then she remembered Lydia's words and thought of the beautiful Miss Masterson. No man was going to make a fool of a Davenant. She had been forced to marry him, but she had no intention of loving him as well. That was not part of the contract, even if preventing herself from doing so was growing harder every hour.

Chapter 11

During the next few days Sarah saw very little of her new husband. They met every evening at dinner and his manner was pleasant and friendly for the benefit of his sister and the servants, but she guessed that behind his affectionate facade he was coldly contemptuous. Dominic, now that his sister was respectably settled and he had a reasonable base for his own activities, was enjoying the life of fashionable society. He spent many hours with his friends and made other new ones and seemed very happy with the arrangement.

Sarah realized that she was the only one not completely contented with their new life. True to his word, the marquess had given her a very generous allowance. The first quarterly payment was more than she had ever had before to spend on herself. Therefore it was easy to accompany Lydia to the shops in Cheapside and the newly fashionable area of Bond Street. No girl could resist the display, and Sarah bought herself fans, ribbons, gloves, slippers, and lengths of silk. She ordered several new gowns and bought some charming hats from the modish milliner patronized by her mother-in-law, the dowager Lady Hawkeworth. All this was very exciting, but underneath her enjoyment Sarah felt an ache, growing daily more painful, that her loveless marriage was going to be very difficult to endure.

Between riding in the park in the marquess's new carriage, shopping, and attending routs and soirées, Sarah had little time to be miserable, particularly with such a lively companion as Lydia. She had not yet, however, caught a glimpse of the famous Miss Masterson.

"She has been indisposed, so Caroline Clinton told me last night at Lady Emworth's," Lydia said cheerfully. "I'm so pleased. I wonder if she knows Gerry has married you. I suppose she must have heard, but I'm sure she is longing to see the lady who has snatched him from under her nose." She giggled wickedly.

Both girls were just preparing for a grand ball at Lady Chesterfield's. Lydia had completed her toilette and come rushing in to supervise Sarah in making the final touches to her own costume.

"Will she be at the ball tonight?" Sarah asked innocently, although her heart began to thump as she waited for the reply.

"I expect so," Lydia murmured, bending over the patch box. "Do you want me to place a patch for you?"

Sarah was sitting in front of her mirror idly regarding her reflection and the youthful style in which Annie had arranged her curls. The powder disguised the brown color, but the yellow of her new formal gown suited her, she thought. Suddenly she caught sight of a tall figure in the mirror and swung around.

"I will place my wife's patch, thank you, Lydia," a voice drawled, and Sarah looked up into the marquess's face. His expression was bland and she could read nothing of his thoughts. This was the first occasion since their marriage more than a week ago that he had come into her bedchamber, and she shivered slightly.

He bent forward and took the box from his sister. With great care he selected a patch in black satin and pressed it carefully to one side of Sarah's mouth. Looking at herself again, she saw it was shaped like a heart,

101

and she caught a challenging glance from the marquess which dared her to object.

"Oh, bravo, Gerry. You have chosen exactly the right one and the place for it!" Lydia exclaimed.

"Well, I have had years of practice," he retorted with a satirical gleam in his dark eyes. "But what I really came in for, my dear, was to give you these." He produced a large, flat case and snapped open the lid.

Inside Sarah saw a beautiful pearl necklace, earrings, and bracelet. The dull sheen of the jewels was milky white and glowing as if with inner radiance. She gazed at them for a long moment.

"Put them on, Sarah, do," Lydia said in excitement. "These are the Hawkeworth pearls, are they not, Gerry? I thought Mama still had them."

"They always pass to the wife of the head of the family," he replied calmly. He put the box on the dressing chest and lifted the necklace out. Deftly he fastened the double string round his wife's neck and stood back to admire them. "They become you," he said quietly. "I hope you will wear the earrings and bracelet as well. I will wait for you both downstairs in the library."

"Oh, but I can't wear these," Sarah objected without thinking. Her hand went to her throat and touched their smoothness.

The marquess had reached the door. He raised his eyebrows, and she was reminded of their first meeting. His hauteur was immense. "You are my wife and will wear them," he stated flatly. "I wish it." He turned and left the room.

"Why don't you want them?" Lydia inquired with real curiosity. "I know Delia Masterson yearned for them and the other Hawkeworth jewels."

"Are there other jewels, then?" Sarah said faintly.

"Of course. They are all yours now except Mama's own personal collection. You are Gerry's wife."

"Yes, I am. Of course. I had not thought of it before. I

102

imagined these should belong to his mother," she said weakly. It was impossible to explain that since the marriage was a farce she had no wish to be decked in jewels that should by rights belong to another.

"Oh, Mama hasn't worn them for years," Lydia said, helping to fasten the earrings. "She thinks pearls suitable for younger ladies. She will be pleased to see you wearing them."

"Then I shall enjoy doing so," Sarah answered quietly.

If Lydia thought it strange her sister-in-law was happy to wear the jewels to please her mother-in-law and not her husband she said nothing. Together both young ladies left the room to join the marquess and Dominic waiting below to escort them to the ball.

It was only a short coach ride from Grosvenor Square down South Audley Street to Chesterfield House. Although built in Mayfair, which caused Sarah a painful reminder of her marriage only a few days before, the mansion was magnificent. The coach deposited them and many other guests by the doors, and, with her hand resting lightly on the marquess's arm, Sarah moved forward into the hallway and gazed at the great marble staircase curving up on either side. Behind them Lydia was chattering to Dominic and seemed unconcerned by her surroundings.

As they mounted the great stairs the marquess, guessing her thought, smiled slightly. "Lydia has been here before, which accounts for her lack of interest," he commented. "I think she will always prefer a handsome young man to a palace however impressive it may be. You will find some of the reception rooms, particularly the blue boudoir, even more splendid, but I prefer the library myself. I hope I shall be permitted to show you around there later on."

Sarah had no time to respond to this before she found herself curtsying to Lord and Lady Chesterfield. Beside her she heard her husband greet the distinguished nobleman and politician with easy familiarity. Looking up, she found herself being scrutinized by her host with frank curiosity.

"So this is your bride, Gerald. She is very lovely and far too good for you. My dear," he said, kissing Sarah's hand, "I congratulate you on captivating this elusive hawk. I feared he would never succumb to a female lure. Did you, my love?" he added, turning to his own wife, who greeted Sarah with dignified friendliness.

They had passed on into a smaller music room and another anteroom before Sarah recovered her composure fully. The marquess stayed beside her for some minutes and introduced her to several fearsome dowagers in towering white wigs and nodding ostrich plumes, friends of his mother's, before disappearing when Jamie St. Clair came up to pay his respects.

"Delighted to see you again," he said with genuine enthusiasm. "Dom has been promising we should become better acquainted for days now. I know we met at the Thatched House Tavern, but one minute you were there, the next you were married and gone. Oh, I beg pardon," he added in some discomfiture, realizing he had not phrased this very well.

Sarah soon put him at ease, for she was used to dealing with her brother, Dominic, and James St. Clair was a similar young man and presented none of the problems she encountered with a sophisticated gentleman like the Marquess of Hawkeworth. They chatted for some minutes, and when the dancing began St. Clair partnered her in a country dance.

As she moved down the set, Sarah looked around for her husband but saw no sign of him. She was not really surprised, since there were at least two hundred guests at the ball spread through various anterooms. She discovered somewhat later that cards were available and many gentlemen had disappeared to gamble the evening away in preference to dancing.

In between sets, Sarah and Lydia sipped lemonade procured for them by Dominic and Jamie. Suddenly

Lydia clutched Sarah's arm and pointed wildly toward a spot where the dancers were once more forming up for the cotillion.

"Look, there is Delia!" she exclaimed. "Now you can see what I mean. She is very pretty, of course, but you have so much more character."

"That is Miss Masterson, is it?" Sarah said dully, watching the gorgeous fair-haired beauty swirl around the ballroom. The girl was dressed in shimmering white silks overlaid with silver gauze, which exactly suited her ethereal fairness and made Sarah feel clumsy and dowdy immediately. But what made her heart sink was Miss Masterson's dancing partner. It did not need Lydia to add in some surprise: "Why, Gerry is dancing with her already! I thought he would have gone to play cards."

Sarah had thought the same, and if he had not then she would have expected him to stand up with her first before seeking out his lady love. Clearly she was wrong; he could not wait to dance with the beauty. Sickened, she turned away to find Sir Peter Trevenning in front of her.

"May I have the pleasure of this dance?" he inquired, smiling down at her.

Recovering her composure, Sarah nodded and gave him her hand. He led her out onto the floor and chatted amiably to her throughout the measures of the dance, so that when it was over she was able to steel herself to meet Miss Masterson calmly enough when the marquess brought her over.

A very few moments in her company decided Sarah that Lydia was right and the girl had beauty but little else. She was taller than Sarah by half a head and wore a very small string of pearls around her neck. Consciousness of her own vastly superior jewels gave Sarah some satisfaction, particularly when she saw Miss Masterson's eyes return to them during the conversation.

"I hope you are quite recovered?" Sarah said politely

as the conversation languished. She had hoped her husband would walk away again, but he was standing close by chatting to Sir Peter and she was certain he was listening to her conversation, or more probably to that of Miss Masterson.

"Oh yes indeed, thank you. I was so very surprised to hear of your sudden marriage when I was able to go about again," Miss Masterson said with ill-concealed curiosity. "Had you known Lord Hawkeworth long? I do not recollect meeting you in London society before."

Her sneer was veiled but nevertheless insulting. Sarah resented the girl's tone but replied sweetly enough. "Ours was a secret romance," she said, sounding as enthusiastic as she could, for the marquess had drawn closer. "We met when Gerald was visiting one of his estates in the country near my home, and I'm afraid it was love at first sight." She fluttered her eyelashes and hid a smile behind her fan.

Miss Masterson looked annoyed, and a tiny frown creased the perfect smoothness of her brow. "Love at first sight for you, no doubt," she agreed. "And for your husband also?" The insinuation was obvious.

Before Sarah could retort, she felt a hand on her arm and a slight warning pressure of the marquess's fingers. "What a question to ask," he said with a laugh. "The perfect wife cannot answer for her husband in such a case. Come, my dear. It is our turn to dance."

Without waiting for her reply, the marquess swung Sarah onto the floor, and she was forced to perform the steps and keep time with him and the music, but she was too angry to be very diplomatic. "You always have an answer, don't you, my lord?" she said crossly.

"The name of the estate you were searching your memory for is Benton," he replied smoothly, ignoring her obvious annoyance. "It lies some twelve miles from Lewes and only about eight miles from your former home. I don't go there often, but very few except my closest associates know that. It will serve our purpose well enough. Otherwise your replies were perfect. However, please try to smile at me. At present you look as if I have abducted you by force, which might be true according to you but is not the view we wish to present to the world. A romance should be portrayed by affection and close attendance to the beloved."

She turned a brilliant smile on him, and he almost missed his step at the change in her. "I congratulate you, my lord. We are now halfway through the evening, and your attendance upon me has been so close this is the first dance we have shared or words we have exchanged. What a model husband! Now don't scowl, my lord," she mocked him. "Although your ill temper is well known, it will never go unremarked and will ruin the romantic image you wish to present."

With a supreme effort he forced down the retort he wished to make and managed to keep his features from betraying his anger. Then the humor of the situation struck him, and he laughed in delight. He had not been wrong in his first impressions of her after all. "Give me leave and I may yet tame you, my little tigress," he murmured, half to himself, as the steps brought them together once more.

Sarah looked up at him in surprise, not sure she had heard him aright, but he was looking over her shoulder, and his good humor had vanished. However, the flash of anger mirrored in his eyes had not been for her and was gone almost at once. As the dance stopped he led her off the floor and over to the spot he had been gazing at.

"Lord Marchmont, may I present my wife, Sarah. Sarah, I am sure you are longing to meet your kinsman," the marquess said. "Wasn't it some great-aunt or other you had in common?"

Sarah found herself face to face with Lord Marchmont, the man she had been so curious about, particularly since her brother, Dominic, had been rude about him. If Dom's story was to be believed, this man had brought about her own misfortunes directly through his own malice. She looked into a pair of cold gray eyes set in a thin, sallow face. The wig he wore was too large, and at once she took offense to the ribbons decorating it in pretty bows, contrasting his effeminate mode of dress with the strong, lithe, muscular figure of the marquess beside her. However, she noticed his eyes were watchful as he bowed over her hand, and his pleasantries did not extend to the expression in them. This is a man to fear, she thought to herself, and was surprised to find she was glad of her husband beside her however ill matched they seemed to be. He would protect her whatever happened, if only to keep his own good name.

"I am delighted to meet you at last. I was devastated not to be at home when you and your brother called on your arrival in town. I might have been able to help you and save you from falling into the difficulties that beset you so shortly afterward."

His words were barbed, and Sarah saw Miss Masterson, who was standing close by, turn at this and move toward them.

"I'm afraid our troubles were purely a family affair," she remarked in honeyed tones. "Dominic had to post off to Sussex so soon after our arrival, our half brother had a seizure, and so he missed my wedding." She hoped fervently that Lord Marchmont did not know poor Thomas.

It seemed he did not. "How sad! I am surprised you didn't wait for his return before marrying, but I suppose after the bet . . ." He left the sentence unfinished.

Deciding to play the silly female to good advantage, Sarah hid behind her fan and trilled with laughter. "Oh yes. So naughty of the pair of them. They did it so well too that everyone thought it was a real bet with me as the stake. So amusing, don't you think? We planned it all the last time Gerald was down at Benton. It seemed so romantic to me, and dear Gerald agreed to humor me. You know how it is when a man is in love," she added, and peeped coyly up at him. It was at this point she noticed the marquess move off with Miss Masterson.

Lord Marchmont's brows had drawn together during her speech, but he managed to nod in a civil way. "Quite so, my lady. Well, I am delighted to have met you at last. You must come to my next soirée. I generally hold one every fortnight. I will send you a card."

"Then you can tell me all about my great-aunt's death," Sarah said to him, and tapped him with her fan. "We were so amazed she had gone. So sudden, wasn't it? And we had never heard her mention you in her letters to dear Papa."

Marchmont murmured something and bowed over her hand. He disappeared in the same direction as that taken by her husband and Miss Masterson. Sarah felt she had acquitted herself well and was pleased she had annoyed him. She could understand Dominic's dislike of him and told him so when he came to claim her for a dance. However, the marquess's defection with the beauty once more had hurt her considerably. She saw no more of him that night, and to make up for his neglect flirted with several of the young men who clamored to dance with her. She spent the supper hour with Sir Peter Trevenning, Lydia, and her brother and tried to believe Sir Peter's assurance that Gerry was playing cards, although she was certain he said this out of kindness.

During the short drive to Grosvenor Square she pretended to be too tired to join in the chatter with Lydia, and the marquess did not encourage her to take part in the conversation.

As they parted at the foot of the stairs the marquess murmured for her ears alone, "It would seem you are experienced in the ways of a man in love. I admire your talent for dissembling, but although it may succeed with Marchmont, remember not to try the same with me."

He had disappeared into his library before Sarah had thought up a retort, and as she climbed the stairs she wondered just how much of her conversation he had heard.

Chapter 12

Several weeks later Sarah decided to take the carriage out to Knightsbridge to see old Nanny and her sister Mary. She had not felt like visiting them before, for she wished to get accustomed to her new mode of life and if possible to reach some understanding with her husband before enduring the scrutiny of Nanny's wise old eyes.

However, matters between herself and the marquess remained much the same. She saw little of him except when they dined at home or if he escorted herself and Lydia to some evening entertainment. At these gatherings he was always polite and attentive, but if Miss Masterson was also present he seemed to spend as much time with her as with his wife. This was hardly a satisfactory state of affairs, but Sarah could see little she could do about it. As she had thought, her own feelings for the marquess had grown stronger and warmer; but she never betrayed her affection for him in private, fearing to be scorned, and in public she kept to her side of the bargain so that people considered them a very loving and affectionate couple. Her only satisfaction in this was that Miss Masterson found these same reports irritating, so Lydia informed her, and the dowager Lady Hawkeworth was growing fond of her, and in return Sarah found herself liking the marquess's mother more at every meeting.

She had duly received a card to a soirée at Lord Marchmont's, but he had avoided spending very long in the company of either of the Davenants, so the mystery surrounding their great-aunt's sudden death and his own inheritance remained a secret, apart from what was generally known.

Sarah was thinking of this as the carriage bowled along the road bringing her, Lydia, and Dominic back from Knightsbridge. Nanny had been delighted to see them all and had scolded Dominic for his naughtiness, although at a warning glance from Sarah had not gone into details of the infamous bet in front of Lydia. The presence of that lively damsel dispelled any restraints Sarah might have felt after her last trip there and also made it very difficult for the old nurse to exchange any private conversation. They had been offered wine and cakes and been generally fussed over, but Sarah had insisted they leave by midafternoon, for she had no wish to incur her husband's displeasure by being late for dinner, particularly when he was going to escort them afterward to a masked ball at Lady Emworth's.

The sun was shining and it was a pleasantly warm May day. Sarah relaxed in her seat and drowsed while Lydia chattered away beside her like a bird, describing the scenery and what she would wear that evening. Dominic was driving, and as the Hyde Park turnpike approached he slowed down to pay the toll.

"Sarah, do wake up and tell me what you intend to wear tonight!" Lydia exclaimed as the carriage slowly moved off again. "I declare I have been talking to you for ten minutes and you have not heard a word I said!"

"I have heard more than one word," Sarah murmured sleepily. "But forgotten them the next minute. I have not decided on what dress to wear, so I cannot tell you, Lydia. Oh! What was that?" she added, sitting upright with a jerk as the coach lurched.

Another sound like a pistol shot echoed around them, and Lydia clutched her sister-in-law's arm in fright. "Someone is shooting at us," she gulped. "What shall we do?"

The coach lurched again and Dominic shouted at the horses, lashing his whip freely around so that they leaped forward and the two girls nearly fell onto the floor. A shot whistled past Sarah's head, and she crouched below the level of the window in sudden terror. Who could be shooting at them, and what for?

"Are we being held up by highwaymen?" Lydia gasped. She attempted to get up, but Sarah held her down.

"Stay beneath the window and you will not be hurt," she whispered. "Dominic will not stop for highwaymen if they are attacking us. He is already speeding up, so we shall soon be safe."

Lydia began to sob as the carriage lurched around a corner at speed, and Sarah prayed they would not overturn. When no further shots came she risked a peep out of the window.

"We can get up now," she said in relief. "We have passed Hyde Park corner and are driving up Tyburn Lane. Soon Dominic will have us back home. Dry your eyes, Lydia."

The girl went on sobbing, as much from excitement as from fright now, but she consented to sit up on the squabs again, and as Dominic's voice was heard singing cheerfully she did dry her eyes and manage a watery smile.

"He regards it as a joke," she murmured in a horrified tone. "How can he?"

"Men are much tougher than we are," Sarah assured her. "Anyway, Dominic loves danger."

"Do you think he was hurt?" Lydia asked suddenly as the carriage lurched again.

Sarah had been wondering the same thing, but quickly

she reassured Lydia. "Of course he wasn't. He would hardly be able to drive us if he had been shot, now would he? Look, we are just about to turn into Grosvenor Square. Dominic can tell us all about it as soon as we are safely inside the house."

She had just finished speaking when the coach drew to a halt with a flourish, and moments later Dominic's face appeared at the window beaming. "I say, that was a splendid drive," he announced cheerfully. "I drove too fast for 'em. Couldn't catch me at all."

"You certainly drove too fast into the square," drawled the marquess. He had observed their approach and now came down the steps toward them as his wife and sister got out of the carriage. "Have you been racing? I wish you would do so in your own curricle and not with any passengers."

"Gerry, we have been attacked," Lydia cried, rushing up to him. "Oh! It was so frightening. I was sure we would be killed."

The marquess's brows rose. Instead of listening to his brother-in-law, who was about to explain, he turned to Sarah for confirmation. "Is this true?"

"I believe so," she said cautiously, beginning to ascend the steps to the door. "We heard what sounded like shots, and one seemed to come through the coach. Dominic must know what happened, since he was driving."

"I'll tell you inside," Dominic said cheerfully. "It was tremendous fun." He took the steps two at a time and disappeared into the hall, but Lydia continued to cling to her brother, although she watched Dominic with admiration in her eyes

"Come into the small salon and tell me all about it," the marquess ordered. "I don't think you three are safe to drive out together. What will you do next?"

"Is that all you can say, Gerry?" Lydia rounded on him. "Don't you care that your sister, your wife, and your brother-in-law were nearly murdered?"

114

"If that were true, I might be concerned," he admitted with a hint of laughter in his voice. "Now, Dominic, stop drinking my best claret and tell me what all this is about."

Dominic drained his glass and threw himself into a chair. "Well, I had just paid the toll at the turnpike before the corner and set m'cattle going again when something whistled past me. It was pretty close and now I come to think of it my coat's been singed. Damn it to hell!" he exclaimed crossly, examining the burnt hole in the twill in dismay. "Why, I bought this only a few days ago. Had it specially made for me."

"Spare us details of your tailor, Dominic, and get on with the story," the marquess murmured, sounding bored. "You had got to the part where you heard something flying past."

"Oh yes. Well, naturally I whipped up the horses, but the stupid beasts were frightened by the noise. Still, they responded well enough."

"We were flung onto the floor," Lydia put in indignantly.

"Probably a good thing, too, since I'm sure a shot went through the coach above my head," Sarah said thoughtfully. She surprised a keen glance from her husband, but he said nothing.

"Is that where it went? Thought the feller missed me but didn't know he was aiming for the coach passengers. Must have been a holdup, though what a place to choose!" Dominic was disgusted. "Who could expect to succeed so close to town?"

"They may not have been mounted but crept out on foot from Shepherd's Market south of Mayfair," the marquess suggested. "Did you see them clearly?"

"No. More's the pity. They could have been mounted or on foot, I suppose. I hadn't thought of them as ordinary thieves from that shabby area. I thought they must be highwaymen."

"As you say, it's too close to London for the usual high toby holdup. Did they shout at you?"

"Never said a word. At least I don't think so." Dominic frowned as he tried to remember. "I was busy with the horses and worried about the girls for a minute or two, then I just enjoyed the fling on the way back," he admitted.

"So I observed," the marquess said dryly. "Well, I doubt if it's anything to worry about." He stood up and took a pinch of snuff, flicking the lace at his wrist delicately. "Probably a new venture by the thieves in that part of the world, and you will have frightened them out of it, I suspect. Such driving as yours would frighten the hardiest of mortals."

Dominic grinned but took the remark in good part. He poured out another glass of wine and began to talk of the horses he wished to purchase next day. Lydia, highly incensed at the way her brother had dismissed the terrifying incident, flounced out of the room. At a signal from her husband, Sarah followed her to try to soothe her, raising her eyes in mock dismay as she went.

That night at Lady Emworth's, Lydia was full of the story, and the horrors they had suffered grew in the telling. Her mother was most concerned and made it her business to approach her son after the unmasking at midnight to inquire what safety precautions he intended to take to stop a recurrence of the incident.

Sarah was listening in some amusement to his skillful explanations and reassurances but found herself cornered by Lord Marchmont. He had noticed her husband was absorbed and took this opportunity of talking to her alone.

"I was so upset to hear of your narrow escape, cousin," he said, bowing over her hand. "I would have come across to express my sympathy for you earlier, but since we were all in disguise I had to wait until the unmasking to be sure I did not pick on the wrong lady."

"It was most kind of you, sir," Sarah said coolly, thinking he probably intended an insult by suggesting he could not recognize her. She knew her lack of stature made her easy to spot in a crowd and the masks only covered the face anyway. She did not betray her irritation with him, and he continued to comment in the same vein.

"Was your carriage stopped?" he asked. "If so it means the villains are becoming damnably daring and we will all have to beware. I could hardly believe my ears when I heard you had been set upon so close to a civilized area of town. One cannot be too careful." He raised a scented wisp of lace to his nose in some agitation.

Concealing her dislike, Sarah agreed with him. "But my husband considers it was probably some criminals from Shepherd's Market, which is not far away. Maybe they feel they can attack traffic on the road, for it is easy to escape into the narrow streets there. They would never be found."

"No indeed. Very shrewd of him. It does not make me feel any easier, though, that such robbers abound in our fair city. Why, I am almost afraid to stay in London!"

"You could always retire to your country estates," another voice broke in, and Sarah was relieved to find her brother had joined them. "What part of the country do you come from, anyway?" Dominic said rather rudely.

Marchmont regarded him coldly. "Yorkshire," he said distantly. "However, I now own estates in Buckinghamshire, but one cannot retire in the middle of the season."

Dominic snorted at this but made no comment. He did refer to Marchmont's other remark. "Estates in Buckinghamshire, eh? I suppose you inherited those from Lady Marchmont a few months ago. Two houses, isn't it?"

"One house, parkland, and farms," Marchmont

117

returned sharply. "Though why you should be interested I don't know. Perhaps you both had hopes of staying there when you first came up to London," he sneered nastily. "You are distant connections, after all, are you not? What was your exact relationship with my aunt?"

"I could ask you the same thing," Dominic said belligerently and jutted out his chin. "I never heard you mentioned until we reached town."

Lord Marchmont bowed. "I find myself in the same position—cousin," he said sweetly, but his eyes were cold. "How strange that one family should know so little about its members. Now if you will excuse me I must take my leave of Lady Emworth." He bowed again over Sarah's hand and left them, mincing along in his high heels and tall wig through the gaily dressed crowd.

"Prancing popinjay," Dominic muttered in disgust. "Feller's a fool, too, for Lady Marchmont had a house and a shooting lodge on the estate besides the farms. I remember from the occasion we stayed there as children. Turns my stomach to think we're related to someone like that. Ugh!"

"Never mind, Dominic. Nobody would believe you were of the same family," the marquess said in his ear. "Otherwise I would not have married your sister, whatever your folly at the gaming tables. But let's rescue my wretched sister Lydia and remove her before she leads all the unsuspecting guests to believe she foiled a masked gang singlehanded!"

Chapter 13

Sarah was not sure what she wanted to believe about the shooting incident. At first she had put it from her mind, dismissing the abortive holdup as just another incident of lawlessness, and one could read about many similar ones every day in the newspapers. She had felt slightly piqued at her husband's lack of interest, but then she could hardly expect him to show acute distress, since he was not in love with her anyway and she had not been hurt. I wonder if he would have been concerned if that shot had hit me, she thought the day afterward. The recollection that she might have left him a widower able to marry the lady he chose did nothing to cheer her, and she resolved not to dwell on the matter at all.

She had other things to think about. Lydia's continued sojourn in her brother's house had brought complications in its wake that Sarah had not foreseen when she had encouraged the girl to come and stay. She had wanted someone to give her an excuse not to be alone with the marquess, but she had forgotten Dominic's presence in the house. He was young and handsome, and it was not surprising Lydia should find him attractive, but Sarah had not bargained for his returning this affection. As the weeks went by and the two were thrown together she noticed their preoccupation with one another and the frequent opportunities Lydia found to go out driving or visiting with Dominic and his willingness to accompany her. She was not the only one to notice this or to be worried by it, as she discovered when the marquess called her into his library one afternoon just as she had returned from a shopping expedition.

"Could you spare me a few moments of your time to discuss a problem?" he asked politely as she crossed the hall.

Sarah could hardly refuse him and indeed had no desire to do so. She regretted her own impulse that had stopped any closer contact between them and hoped that perhaps she could now make amends for her former abruptness. It was the first occasion in weeks that he had desired to see her alone, and she welcomed the opportunity.

He held the door open for her to pass through and then followed her into the room. She noticed he was dressed for riding in fawn breeches, brown twill coat, and polished top boots. He wore no wig, and his hair was unpowdered and drawn back into a bow at the neck. Glad she had on her new gown of apple-green dimity, Sarah untied her cloak and bonnet and threw them into a chair before turning to smile at him.

"How can I help you, sir?" she asked pleasantly.

"First I would like to thank you for arranging flowers in here every day. It is your hand that is responsible, I'm sure."

"Yes indeed. I felt that a bowl of spring flowers would make the room just perfect when I first saw it," she admitted, "and I dared to try it and see. The result was so successful, and you did not object, so I have continued the practice. I found the chance to slip in here and browse among the books very welcome too," she added wistfully.

"Surely the round of fashionable life is not too tiring for you?"

"Oh no, indeed not, but I like to be alone sometimes, sir," she said hurriedly.

"I, too," he agreed. "Do you think you might also call me by my name, or would that be stretching our bargain too far? I find that being called sir or referred to always by some indirect honorific is extremely aging."

Her dimple appeared and she smiled shyly. "I will certainly try, Gerald."

"Good. I hope that you will go on trying even after I have talked to you. I fear you might not care for what I am about to say, but I cannot help that. Can I pour you a glass of ratafia?"

"No, thank you. Go on with what you have to say. I am intrigued." She sat down, and after he had poured himself some wine he threw himself into a nearby chair and stretched his booted feet toward the empty grate.

"I think it is time Lydia returned to Mama," he began rather too abruptly. "She has been here for more than a month and is monopolizing you far too much."

Sarah regarded him in surprise. "She is no trouble at all, sir—Gerald, I mean. We get on very well. Please do not send her home on my account. I'm afraid she will be very disappointed if you do send her back."

"She cannot spend all her life here," he said irritably.

"A couple of months in one season is hardly a lifetime," Sarah put in dryly. "Do you have some other reason for sending her back to live with Lady Hawkeworth?"

He looked straight at her and nodded. "You are shrewd. I thought you would ask me that question. Although I am sure you will object to my answer. I do have another reason, and that, as you have probably guessed, is your brother, Dominic."

Sarah had been expecting this, but she watched him coolly. "Lydia is young and impressionable," she suggested calmly. "Is that what worries you?"

"Yes, it is. That and Dominic's ineligibility. Don't get annoyed with me," he added, getting up and beginning to pace the floor. "I have to think of Lydia's future, and your brother has nothing to offer her, no fortune, no prospects, only a handsome face."

"Totally ineligible, as I was, so therefore he must stand by and let you ruin his life," she said bitterly.

"Hardly that. He will still see Lydia, but not so much, and I hope she will meet other suitors."

"And forget my brother," Sarah flared up. "Of course. I would have expected you to feel like that. To be saddled with one Davenant in the family is enough; two would be intolerable. Is that it?" She got to her feet and gazed up at him stormily.

His rueful and apologetic expression immediately changed. He looked down at her haughtily. "However you wish to phrase it, Dominic is not a suitable husband for my sister Lydia. She must return to her mother, and I hope you will not encourage them to meet more than is absolutely necessary." His tone was cold.

"I will not need to encourage them. Separation is just the spark that is needed to fan their affection for each other into something more permanent. I am surprised you cannot see that for yourself. If left alone, their interest in one another will probably fade away, but send Lydia home and she will defy you."

"You clearly do not know Lydia. A Hawkeworth does not behave so," he snapped. "I can see you are not prepared to be reasonable about this, as I feared. Well, she will return to my mother on Saturday. It is now Wednesday and she has two days to pack her belongings. You may tell her so, and I will speak to her later." He moved to the door, but Sarah was before him.

122

"Your obedient servant, sir," she said contemptuously, curtsied, and left him.

Lydia was as upset and indignant as Sarah had expected. She called her brother many names, and Sarah hid a smile. If the marquess could see Lydia now he would hardly credit such behavior to a Hawkeworth, she thought. When told this, Lydia gave a watery smile and sniffed.

"He has no idea what it is to be in love," she sobbed, resorting to tears. "If he had ever been moved by tender feelings he would never separate us. How can he be so cruel?"

"You are only going back to your mama's," Sarah said sensibly. "You can still see Dominic almost every day at balls and parties."

"Not if Gerry has his way, you see," Lydia said, her tears drying with the return of her anger. "He will watch me and interfere. Oh, I hate him!"

"You mustn't say that," Sarah murmured. "He has your best interests at heart. But why don't you go and see him yourself? You might be able to persuade him to wait another week or two at least."

Lydia sprang up from her bed, where she had thrown herself in her misery. "Oh yes. I will go now and see if I can wheedle a few more weeks out of him. If he would only stop thinking about the future. Now he is married he wants me safely settled with some suitable but so dull partner who is rich and probably old as well."

She flounced out of the room, and, sighing, Sarah followed her, but did not go downstairs. She retired to her own chamber and wondered if Lydia's casual words could refer to her own marriage too. Did her husband feel he was safely settled to someone dull and could now enjoy himself somewhere else? It was very likely, and even more depressing than his rudeness about the ineligibility of the Davenants, for she knew this to be true. Poor Dominic had no expectations, and Sarah wondered what he would do when he discovered the marquess did not approve of him in connection with his sister.

She heard nothing that evening, for Dominic was out with friends attending a prizefight outside London, and Lydia could not tell him what had occurred. Sarah had to endure her sulks throughout dinner and her refusal to accompany their party to the play at the theater in Drury Lane afterward, which put the marquess out of temper as well.

Hoping that the next two days would not be filled with scenes and sulks, Sarah dressed for a ridotto at Ranelagh the following evening with mixed feelings. She had almost expected her husband to withdraw his consent to the expedition, since he himself was not coming with them. He had an engagement for cards but had permitted Dominic to offer his escort with Jamie St. Clair. Sarah had seen little of her brother on his return that morning but she knew he had been closeted with Lydia for an hour or more in the gold salon while the marquess was out riding and felt she should have intervened.

When she set out in their company she was amazed to find them both cheerful and apparently without a care in the world. This was so surprising after Lydia's sulks that Sarah immediately became suspicious and wondered what they could be plotting between them.

However, since this was her first visit to Ranelagh she was determined not to allow her worries to spoil the pleasure. The gardens had only been opened a few years before, and even the king occasionally graced the place with his presence, for he enjoyed a romp now and again. The shady walks were lit by colored lamps here and there, and the huge rotunda, pride of the gardens for its immense size of over two hundred feet, was ablaze with candles. Impressed by the scene and delighted with everything she saw, Sarah prepared to enjoy herself and forget her problems for one evening.

Dominic had secured them a box and ordered supper. After they had eaten he suggested taking a turn around the gardens to admire the fountains and enjoy the walks between the avenues of trees. Lydia agreed excitedly, and Sarah also nodded with enthusiasm. But mindful that her husband trusted her to keep an eye on his sister, she refused to allow them to wander away alone.

Lydia appeared to accept this and linked her arm with Sarah's and chatted happily to St. Clair and Dominic, not favoring one man or the other. She was dressed in a deep-golden-colored domino which hid her paler silken gown underneath and covered her curls. Since they all wore masks, Sarah began to wonder if her brother had made plans for later in the evening and determined to stay as close to Lydia as possible whatever happened, since it would be easy to lose anyone in the crowds, particularly among people wearing masks.

"I say, I think that man wants to speak to me," Dominic murmured a moment later as they all stood admiring the fountains. "Must be George. Said he was coming tonight, and I asked him to join us, and Marchmont, too."

"Oh no, you didn't? Dominic, how could you?" Sarah objected at once. "You know I dislike Lord Marchmont exceedingly."

"So do I," put in Lydia promptly. "He is always overdressed and minces about on such ridiculous high heels. I hope he falls over, but only if I am there to watch." She giggled.

Dominic was waving wildly to a man in a green domino, who waved back. "Must be George," he said. "Excuse me."

"Wait, Dominic! Why did you ask Marchmont to join us?" Sarah demanded.

Dominic paused and shrugged his shoulders. "Didn't ask him, really. We all met in the Cocoa Tree the night before the prizefight, didn't we, Jamie? I was talking about the ridotto and he said he would be here tonight and would join us. Couldn't really refuse without sounding rude. Must go," he added and moved off into the crowd.

"Feller was trying to be pleasant," Jamie St. Clair excused his friend. "Don't like him myself, either, but then I don't know anyone who does," he admitted, sounding puzzled at this. "But he is related to Dom, after all, in a vague way, y'know."

Sarah was not mollified and guessed her brother must have been in his cups to have proffered such an invitation at all. Lydia consoled her with her usual optimism. "He could never find us among all these people," she said cheerfully. "We might recognize him with his topheavy wig and heels even if he wears a domino, but he would never notice us."

"No. You're quite right," Sarah agreed. "Anyway, I can't imagine him coming to such a party as this. Shall we walk down to the temple at the end of this avenue and then return to the rotunda for the dancing? I'm sure Dominic will have caught us up by then."

They wandered off happily and spent their time admiring all they could see and trying to guess who was concealed under various dominoes as they passed by. They reached the rotunda again and seated themselves, but Dominic did not join them.

For a while none of them was unduly worried, but when a green domino appeared and threw back his hood cheerfully Sarah felt vaguely uneasy.

"Hallo, George," Jamie greeted him "Where's Dom? Is he following you?"

"Dom?" George Henderson said, looking around as if he expected his friend to appear from behind him. "I left him hours ago. Said I'd join you later, but he was on his way back, so I thought he would be here too. Have you lost him?"

"He's probably met someone else and stopped to chat," Jamie said without surprise. "He has no idea of time."

"You left him hours ago?" Sarah queried.

"Well, an hour or so, I should think," George amended. "Jamie's right, though. He must have seen another friend. Will be here soon. Can I join you?" He bowed, and Lydia giggled naughtily as his green domino flopped into his eyes.

She was happy enough to dance with him a few minutes later and reassured Sarah that her brother would return. "He promised me a surprise at midnight," she whispered confidentially. "Now don't disapprove, dear Sarah. Just pretend you didn't hear, but he will be back by then. Dance with Jamie and stop worrying."

"That's right. Dance with me, my lady," Jamie agreed. "Don't want to worry about old Dom. What could happen in a place like this?"

Yet several hours later, after the unmasking at midnight, even the sanguine Jamie was looking perturbed, and Lydia began to sob noisily. "He promised me, he promised," she said wildly. "Where is he?"

"I'll go and look," Jamie said, and George agreed with alacrity. Neither young gentleman wished to be left with a distraught young lady, and they soon disappeared in the crowd while Lydia's sobs grew louder, and Sarah decided she must take the girl home before they attracted any more attention. Already she could feel many pairs of eyes riveted to the box where she sat trying to calm her sister-in-law, but to no avail. She was greatly relieved to hear her husband's voice and to see his arrogant face gazing down at them.

"Stop that noise, Lydia, and control yourself," he said peremptorily. "You are attracting unwelcome attention. What is the fuss about, anyway?"

Lydia hiccuped and choked herself into a sniffling silence, and Sarah replied as calmly as she could. "Dominic left us to talk to a friend several hours ago, but he never returned," she explained. "His friend joined us, and we have had his company until he and Mr. St. Clair went off to search the grounds. Dominic has just disappeared."

"Nonsense," he said abruptly. "He might have left you, but I doubt if he has disappeared."

"He would never leave me all evening," Lydia put in and seemed about to cry again.

Hawkeworth glared at her, and she buried her face in a tiny handkerchief. "I can imagine him leaving you both if you make displays like this. No doubt your other escorts have been unable to endure it either," the marquess said coldly. "Did it not occur to you that in a place this size with so many people milling about Dominic probably thought he had lost track of you and decided to await you at my house in Grosvenor Square? Any sensible man would do that. Come along now. I have had my coach brought around to the back entrance, since I dislike taking the ferry on the river. I will escort you home."

"Thank you," Sarah said, standing up and helping Lydia to her feet. "If you direct us to the coach, we can go alone and need not spoil your evening, sir." Her gaze was challenging, and he did not meet her eyes.

Instead he turned around and merely offered her his arm. From the corner of her eye as she took it Sarah saw a lady standing nearby whisk around and conceal herself behind a pillar, but not before she had recognized that fair hair and beautiful face. So the Masterson was here with her husband, and that was why he had not accompanied them. So much for trusting him and believing in the card party. Stiffly she walked along beside him and kept her arm around Lydia consolingly. Dominic might well be waiting for them in Grosvenor Square, but by his disappearance he had exposed the marquess for the deceiver he was. She knew she should feel angry and disgusted, but her heart ached and she felt cold and lonely. At least Lydia cared for Dominic and he for her, but nobody would mourn her disappearance, and the thought was chilling.

Chapter 14

The coach ride back to Grosvenor Square was an uncomfortable one. Lydia sniffled and sobbed in one corner of the carriage beside Sarah, and the marquess sat alone and occasionally barked at his sister, ordering her to control herself. In the light from the odd flare held by a passing linkboy on the road, Sarah saw his face was forbidding and guessed he was regretting the ruination of his evening with Miss Masterson. She was tempted to chide him about the girl but decided now was not the moment. She was also too worried about her brother to spare much thought for her own problems.

When they reached the house, Sarah's worries increased. There was no sign of Dominic, and the butler informed his master that young Mr. Davenant had not returned since he had set out with the ladies earlier. This sent Lydia into hysterics, and Sarah and her maid had difficulty calming her down. Eventually they managed to get the girl into bed and give her a soothing draught to help her relax. She implored Sarah to sit with her, and she did so until Lydia fell asleep worn out with crying.

Sarah herself was glad of Annie's posset, but slept only fitfully. Recurrent dreams of shooting and a nightmare chase in a coach ruined her slumber, and she woke early unrefreshed. After dressing quickly in an old blue cotton gown without a hoop under her skirts, Sarah slipped along to see how Lydia fared. She found the girl still deeply asleep and told the maid to leave her as long as possible.

Early as she was, she found the marquess had already breakfasted when she reached the dining room. However, he stayed and drank another cup of coffee with her while she nibbled at some bread and butter with little appetite.

"Don't worry about him," the marquess advised her calmly after he had informed her Dominic was still away. "Surely he used to go off for nights at a time when you lived in Sussex? If you always worried yourself into a state like this I would be surprised."

"Life was different in Sussex," Sarah defended herself. "Of course Dominic went off and stayed away, as you say, but I usually knew where he was even if he didn't tell me. Anyway, my father was alive, and therefore the problem and responsibility were not mine. I merely had to smooth the way for him so that Papa did not get too upset."

The marquess smiled. "Why should last night be any different from those in Sussex?" he asked.

Sarah sipped her coffee thoughtfully. "He was escorting Lydia and me, and he would never have neglected the duties of a host. His manners are too good for that. Something must have happened to him."

"He could have fallen into the low company of some friends, imbibed too much wine, and been too ashamed to return to you girls," Hawkeworth suggested.

Sarah turned to him eagerly. "Oh, do you think that's possible? I should be most annoyed with him if he did so, but at least it is a reasonable explanation."

"There is bound to be a good explanation for his absence, whatever you might think to the contrary." The marquess put down his empty cup and got to his feet. He strolled across to the door. "I have sent around to all the places he might have been taken if he was in an inebriated state last night, and we should hear soon. If not, he will probably come in having spent the night with a friend and be surprised at your concern."

"I'm sure you are right, sir," she said with a sigh. "I wish I could believe you. I will do my best to try." She also got up from the table. "If it were not for Lydia I'm sure you would be right."

"You mean they arranged last night's outing for a purpose?" he demanded, pausing halfway through the door.

"Oh no, nothing like that, I assure you," she said defensively, but felt herself flushing rosily as she remembered Lydia's confidences about what Dominic had promised. "It was just a masquerade, but I believe my brother's feelings are too deeply committed to your sister for him to hurt her wantonly by such rude and careless behavior as you suggest."

The marquess's frown disappeared at this, but he nodded. "That is the only aspect of the affair which puzzled me," he admitted, to her surprise. "But I'm certain there will be a rational explanation. Now I am going out. You would be wise to take some fresh air yourself—a walk in the park, perhaps?"

"Oh, no. I must wait for news," Sarah insisted.

Her husband shrugged. "As you wish," he said in a bored tone. He crossed the hall and received his hat and cane from a footman, then the butler ushered him outside.

Sarah wandered slowly upstairs, wishing she could think of some occupation to take her mind off Dominic. She was irritated by the marquess's indifference and decided he must be piqued because her brother's disappearance had upset his own plans. This was no more consoling than her other thoughts, and she paced the floor of the green salon impatiently.

For the next hour her temper grew more strained.

She attempted to settle to some embroidery but could not set the stitches and flung the frame aside. A book went the same way, for she lacked concentration. When at last she heard the sound of an arrival below, she rushed to the head of the stairs, eagerly hoping there would be news of Dominic at last.

There was. As she ran down to the hall, ignoring the butler's disapproval, she saw Jamie St. Clair helping a disheveled figure along, and following behind was the marquess.

"Take him into the library," Hawkeworth ordered crisply. "See that we are not disturbed, Carton," he added to the butler. "Not by anybody. But first bring wine and biscuits."

"I would prefer some cold sirloin," the tattered figure croaked cheerfully, and Sarah recognized her brother. She rushed forward and took his other arm as they moved into the book-lined sanctuary.

"You can have some later, and ham and eggs as well," the marquess said, and grinned. "But first I want some explanations. My wife has been upset, my sister reduced to hysterics and the creation of scenes in a public place, while I have had to put up with it all."

Sarah shot him a look of reproach, which he ignored. She helped her brother into the marquess's own seat near the fireplace and gazed at him in some bewilderment. St. Clair shuffled his feet nervously and looked towards the marquess with some trepidation. He said nothing in answer to Sarah's excited questions, and nor did Dominic until the butler had made his stately way back with the refreshments.

When the four of them were alone, Dominic pushed back his disordered hair and regarded his dirty evening clothes in some disgust. His actions disclosed an enormous bruise above his eye, and Sarah exclaimed again, only this time in horror.

"What has happened to you, Dominic?" she cried. "You must tell us at once, for I can't endure the suspense any longer. How do you come to be in that state? Where have you spent the night? With Mr. St. Clair?"

"Oh no, ma'am. Not with me," Jamie said quickly. "Sent for me this morning to bail him out, that's all."

Sarah looked puzzled, and Dominic laughed at her expression. The marquess was standing over by the window gazing into the garden, but his shoulders shook slightly, and she knew he was laughing at her too.

"Tell me what has happened," she demanded. "You all seem to know except me, and I cannot see what you have to laugh at either."

Hawkeworth turned around. "Explain yourself, Davenant. I appreciate the difficulties, but we are all curious. Which lockup was it you spent the night in, by the way?"

"Lockup? Do you mean prison?" Sarah was aghast.

"It was the Roundhouse, actually," Dominic told them, and Jamie nodded his head. "I was pulled in by the Watch for being drunk and behaving in a disorderly manner, or so they said. I can't remember, myself." Again he rubbed his head, but a pull or two at the drink steadied him.

The marquess raised his eyebrows mockingly at Sarah, and she found herself irritated to think he was right once more.

"Sent for me this morning," put in St. Clair again, helpfully. "Asked me to go and pay the fine so he could get out. Of course I did," he added.

"I'll reimburse you, old fellow," Dominic muttered. "Oh, how my head hurts!"

"That pleasure will be mine," said the marquess, feeling in his pockets. "But you still have some explaining to do."

Sarah had subsided into a seat but looked up at this. "Yes, Dominic. Why did you leave us at Ranelagh?" she asked. "You were supposed to join us in the rotunda. Where did you go?"

"I don't know," he admitted. "I went across and spoke to George, as you saw. Then I left him, and he promised to join us later."

"He did," St. Clair agreed.

"Did he? Good fellow, George. Must have wondered where I'd got to, I expect."

"We all wondered," Sarah snapped, her patience going fast.

"Just tell us what happened," the marquess added gently, "before we expire with curiosity." His wife knew he was laughing again, but his expression betrayed nothing.

"That's the trouble. I can't explain," Dominic complained. "I turned around to walk back to the rotunda, and that was it. Wham! I was finished."

"What do you mean?"

The marquess took pity on Sarah and told her. "He was knocked out, I gather—removed from the gardens and dumped somewhere near St. Giles, where the Watch found him and took him to the lockup—in this case, the Roundhouse—to cool his heels until morning."

"That must have been it," Dominic agreed in relief. "I do remember hazily that I was in a street and somebody was shouting at me. Then I was grabbed and I can remember little else until I woke this morning in that dreadful hole. I shouldn't like to be a criminal," he added reflectively. "There were rats in the place, and the straw on the floor was disgusting. No food either," he added, draining his second glass of wine.

The marquess thoughtfully removed the bottle from his reach. "You had better go and clean up, then have a good breakfast," he suggested sensibly. "It's nearly noon, and if you drink much more of my claret you will be well and truly drunk now even if you were sober enough last night. Maybe St. Clair will be good enough to help you upstairs, although he might not want to get too close to you," he added, wrinkling up his nose.

"Don't mind at all," St. Clair volunteered. "Well, not

very much. You do smell awful, old feller," he was heard to murmur as they left the room. "Have to burn these clothes, y'know."

"Burn them!" shouted the enraged Dominic, recovering some of his old vigor. "But this is a new coat, I'll have you know, Jamie. Only had it delivered yesterday."

"Must go all the same, Dom." Jamie's voice faded away as they moved up the staircase. "Torn as well."

The marquess closed the door on Dominic's grumbles, and there was no doubt he was laughing now. "I think your brother has survived his ordeal and will suffer no lasting harm apart from a slight headache," he reassured Sarah. "If he can think of nothing more than his damaged coat, he'll do."

"Yes, but why did he get attacked at all?" Sarah asked. "Who would want to harm him?"

"Do you know of anyone?" Hawkeworth asked her.

"No, I don't. Dominic never had any enemies in Sussex as far as I know, and he has been in London only a few weeks. Surely he cannot have upset anyone so much they would have had him attacked?"

"It is unlikely," the marquess agreed. "What I suspect is that he was mistaken for someone else. After all, you were all in dominoes, were you not? He was hit by some thugs and removed, and the mistake discovered too late, so instead of finishing him off he was left for the Watch to find. He was lucky."

Sarah shivered. "Lucky!"

"A night's discomfort and a bruised head. The man the blow was intended for would probably be dead by now," the marquess said in a matter-of-fact tone. "Stop worrying and forget the incident. I am certain it was a case of mistaken identity. Dominic has a hard head and will be none the worse for the experience. Most young men spend a night or so in a place like the Roundhouse at some time or other. Let's hope this will be his only night there."

"Did you?" she asked before she could stop herself.

He flicked her cheek lightly with a finger. "I must not divulge the follies of my youth. Go and waken my sister and tell her the good news that the wanderer has returned."

Chapter 15

Lydia was so relieved to find Dominic safely returned with only a bruise to show for his adventure that for the rest of the day she forgot all about her imminent departure for home and instead followed him around. Sarah was quite glad when Dominic decided to try out a new pair of horses, and Lydia persuaded him to take her along for the ride. In another day Lydia would be back with her mama, and Sarah thought no harm could come of their spending a few hours in each other's company. She was prepared to defend her action in allowing them to go off to the marquess if he asked, but once Dominic was safely in the house he had disappeared and she had no idea when he intended to return.

Relieved of her anxieties and for once without any social engagements, Sarah spent a pleasant afternoon at home. She organized the maids to begin the task of packing Lydia's belongings and spent a happy hour trying on several new hats and bonnets she had purchased a few days before. She was just thinking of beginning to dress for dinner when a footman knocked on her chamber door and delivered a letter which had been brought around by special messenger.

"Is he waiting for an answer?" Sarah asked as she picked up the sheet of notepaper.

"No, my lady," he replied woodenly.

"But it's addressed to my brother!" she exclaimed, turning it over.

"Yes, my lady, but I brought it to you because the messenger said on no account was Lord Hawkeworth to see it," the footman said stolidly. He looked straight ahead of him, and his expression remained impassive.

Sarah turned the letter over in her hands. "I see," she said in a noncommittal tone. "Then I will give it to him myself. You may go."

"Thank you, my lady."

"Say nothing of this to anyone, John," she added to his departing back.

"No, my lady," he murmured and closed the door behind him.

Once more alone in her bedchamber, Sarah wondered what she should do. If this was a private message, as it appeared to be, she ought to keep it safely until Dominic returned. But the method of delivery was strange. Why send a messenger openly to hand over a private note that must on no account be seen by the owner of the house? It seemed very odd. Perhaps it was some kind of joke, she thought. The paper was ordinary enough and not like the thick, expensive paper used by her husband. As she stood irresolute, tapping it in her hands, she noticed the wafer sealing the back was loose. It took only a moment to prise this up and open the paper out.

"I can always pretend I thought it was addressed to me," she said to herself and started guiltily as Annie bustled into the bedchamber and disappeared into the adjoining dressing room.

The note was short. It read: "I hold your bill for £500, which has been outstanding for two weeks now. This is a debt of honour, and I must have repayment tomorrow at noon. I will be waiting at the Swan with Two Necks,

Lad Lane. Your future will suffer if you fail to be there."

The note was unsigned.

Sarah crumpled it between her fingers as Annie came back into the room. She stuffed it out of sight behind a chest when Annie's back was turned and allowed herself to be dressed without joining in the usual chatter.

"You're quiet tonight, Miss Sarah," Annie murmured—she always forgot to call her mistress by her new title. "I thought you would be so happy with Master Dominic back again."

"Oh, I am, Annie," Sarah agreed absentmindedly. The words of that note were fixed in her mind, but the meaning was less clear. Was the writer a tradesman or a gentleman? It was hard to tell, since a bill for £500 could mean either, and yet a debt of honour was mentioned. As the meeting place was at some tavern, Sarah had no idea where it was or if this signified anything. What should she do about it? Her first thought had been to slip along to her brother's suite of rooms on the floor above and give it to him. But she was not sure if this was the sensible thing to do, since she knew he was very short of cash. The purchase of clothes and a new pair of matched grays had cut deeply into his slender resources, yet she herself had more money than she could possibly spend in a quarter. The marquess had been so generous, and she had almost that sum in the house put aside to pay the milliner's huge bill. She could use this money for Dominic easily, but she was certain he would refuse to take it if she suggested such a thing. He was so proud and would spoil what chances he had for the future with Lydia or any other well-dowered girl if he was involved in another scandal. This thought clinched the matter. She would go herself to this meeting place and pay the money she had and promise the rest at the beginning of next week, when she could draw on her remaining allowance at the bank.

With her decision made, Sarah felt much calmer. Annie had finished arranging her hair and now covered her gown with the powdering robe and put the finishing touches to the style with a light dusting of powder. She was pleased with the effect and stood back to admire her mistress in her cream satin gown with the bodice of lace and full flowing sleeves. However, Sarah sensed she was in disgrace for being so quiet.

"You must forgive me, Annie, but I have been very tired. I slept little for worrying last night."

Annie's face relaxed, and she smiled in sympathy. "Of course you didn't. Who could, with the master missing? Just you try and come to bed early for a change."

"I would love to, Annie." Sarah sighed. "But we are engaged for a rout party at the Chathams' and cannot disappoint them."

"A pity," Annie snorted. "Still, you will not disgrace me. No one could look lovelier. That topaz necklace and bracelet go very well with the gown," she added critically. "But I wish you would wear the emerald or the sapphire set from those jewels his lordship gave you."

"I feel uncomfortable in heavy family jewelry," Sarah excused herself. "These were my mother's own, and I prefer them." She picked up her fan and gloves, and Annie knew better than to say any more.

Lydia and Dominic were also of the party going to the Chathams', and Sarah was pleased to see the marquess ignore them both and the fact they spent the best part of the evening together. She wondered if he would have been so forbearing if he had known of Dominic's debt and the latest threat of scandal connected with the family. Her own pleasure in the evening was marred by the prospect of the meeting next day, and she had told Annie the truth when she had pleaded her tiredness. Even her husband commented on her quiet demeanor, and she was forced to make the same excuse to him, which he accepted just as readily as the maid had done.

Feeling guilty at her deception but relieved too, Sarah was glad when the marquess ordered the carriage brought around at midnight.

"The evening has only just begun, Gerry," Lydia complained at once when told they were returning to Grosvenor Square. "If Sarah is tired, take her home and send the carriage back for us," she pleaded.

"What a selfish child you are," Hawkeworth said, but in a kindly tone. "You think only of your own pleasure. Consider how poor Dominic spent last night, and where. He will agree to stay with you, I'm sure, but would probably prefer his own bed."

"Oh, of course. I had forgotten," Lydia exclaimed, looking guilty. "Forgive me, Dominic. Certainly we must go back at once."

Dominic made a halfhearted protest, saying he would stay if she wished, but seemed ready to leave when Lydia, now full of remorse, insisted they make their farewells immediately.

As she swept off, almost dragging him into the carriage, the marquess laughed to himself. He led his wife after them and murmured mischievously: "Just see what wonders imagining herself in love can work on my empty-headed sister. Maybe we should try it sometime."

"Do you have such an imagination?" Sarah asked in surprise.

He looked down at her enigmatically. "Maybe I was hoping you did," he suggested. He showed her so much solicitous attention on the journey back to the house she was overwhelmed and wished she had not got a guilty conscience which prevented her from acting as naturally as she would have wished.

Next morning she again woke early with a sinking feeling in the pit of her stomach. However, she had resolved to go in place of Dominic and made her preparations accordingly. She had spent quite a while in the night hours wondering if she should dress in the disguise of a young man so that nobody would recognize her, but she decided against it in the morning light. It would present almost insuperable difficulties for her in leaving the house in Grosvenor Square. She could imagine the servants' surprise, and even worse, there was the possibility she might meet her husband or brother while on her way to the street. It would be beyond her understanding to invent a plausible excuse for appearing in men's breeches, and the marquess, at least, would know she was up to something he would not approve of.

So she chose to dress in one of her plainest gowns, with only the smallest hoop and no embroidery or lace trimming. It was an old garment she had brought with her from Sussex, and Annie seemed surprised when her mistress asked for it and one of her drab cloaks to cover it.

"Why do you want to wear that old thing?" the maid asked at once. "You have so many pretty gowns now to choose from."

"That doesn't mean I have to discard all my other clothes," Sarah said tartly. "But I do have a good reason. If you remember, Miss Lydia is returning to her mother's house today and I have promised to go along too this afternoon, and you know how much luggage she has."

"I do indeed," agreed Annie, diverted by this. "I have never seen so many bandboxes and bags all for one young lady."

"So you see I have no wish to spoil one of my new gowns helping her," Sarah said and smiled. She tucked her well-filled reticule into a large pocket in the skirt of the gown and folded the cloak over her arm. It was a dark-blue color and shabby enough to cause comment if the marquess should see her wearing it, so she had decided to carry it until she was safely out of the house.

In the hall the only person there was the footman, and Sarah hoped she would be able to go out without seeing anyone, but suddenly the small salon door opened and Lydia appeared.

"Where are you going, Sarah?" she asked at once. "Do you want me to accompany you?"

"Oh no," Sarah replied quickly. "I will not be long. I promised to visit an old servant who lives nearby, but I will be back for nuncheon and then we will take the carriage around to your mother's house."

Lydia made a face and sighed, but a voice from inside the room recalled her attention and she returned to Dominic, probably to make the most of her last few hours in his company, Sarah thought guiltily as she stole away.

She had decided to take a hackney carriage to the tavern named in the letter, since she had no idea where this might be. It was only eleven o'clock, so she thought there should be plenty of time to reach the place, wherever it was. She found a hackney in South Audley street and was glad to sink into the rather grubby interior, for she had been afraid of being recognized walking along even in her shabby cloak. The driver had looked surprised when she asked to be taken to the Swan with Two Necks in Lad Lane, but after telling her it was a tidy trot into the city he had agreed.

As the horses trotted along High Holborn and into the city past Newgate Prison, Sarah grew more nervous. She had no idea who she was expecting to see, and it suddenly occurred to her that neither would the writer of the letter know or recognize her. He would be expecting her brother, and she might find it very difficult to make contact with him. She never for a moment thought of the writer as being a woman. The carriage rumbled on, the driver shouting loudly at a carter who was blocking the roads ahead while the shouts of street traders mingled with the sound of church bells striking twelve.

Sarah sat up and looked out of the window. She fidgeted with the hood of her cloak, which she had

144

drawn over her hair, and wondered if they had far to go, for she did not wish to be late for the meeting. Already they had passed St. Paul's Church and were rolling up Wood Street. In another moment the hackney turned into a narrow lane and pulled up at the tavern. A creaky sign hung outside showing a most peculiar white bird with two heads, presumably the Swan with Two Necks, she thought as she handed the driver a crown, to his evident delight.

"Thankee, ma'am, thankee kindly," he called after her. "If you should be needing a ride back, just call on me. I'll be here a while yet."

Sarah murmured her gratitude and hoped she would be able to return with him very shortly, for this inn was not as clean or pleasant a place as she had hoped. The yard was dirty, and she was only just able to avoid the plunging hooves of a highly bred horse being backed into a lightweight racing carriage. Her foot slipped in the mud, and she was grateful to reach the door into the taproom, which seemed filled with many noisy, hard-drinking men with no sign of a gentleman among them.

She was standing there nervously wondering what to do when she heard her name spoken.

"My dear Lady Hawkeworth—or should I say, cousin Sarah—what a pleasure to see you."

She turned around, and to her dismay found herself facing the elegant, foppishly attired figure of Lord Marchmont. He was holding a lace handkerchief to his nostrils to lessen the odor of dung and sweat and looked even more out of place than she did.

"Lord Marchmont. What a surprise," she managed to say.

"You must let me take you into a private parlor, if I can secure one, and procure you some refreshment," he offered.

"Oh no. No, I couldn't," she stammered quickly. "You

see, I am meeting someone here, and I must not miss this person."

Lord Marchmont's eyebrows rose toward his elaborate wig, which was a curtly brown one this morning. "I see. What an unusual place for a rendezvous, if I may say so." He tittered unpleasantly. "Do I know the gentleman?"

Sarah was furious with herself for not thinking of some good excuse for her presence in this place, but she cursed her luck that of all people she should meet this odious man, who would be bound to talk about it. "I am afraid I am not at liberty to indulge in names," she said firmly, hoping to quell his curiosity.

She was unlucky. His beady eyes were bright, and he even endured being pushed by a rough yokel anxious to gain the taproom, so eager was he to hear more. "An assignation, no doubt?" he asked at once.

"Not of the sort you mean," she snapped without thinking. Then, realizing it would do no good to antagonize him, she added, "I have a business matter to attend to. You must excuse me. The meeting is merely to settle a small bill."

"Ah," he breathed at once. "I see."

Sarah made to move into the inn, for she preferred the rough customers to this inquisition which could only affect her badly afterward. She had mentioned a bill, for it was the truth, and would be better than a story about an assignation with a lover which he would probably spread otherwise.

To her surprise he took hold of her arm, and his grip was surprisingly strong. "Come and sit in my carriage while you wait," he said in a kindly tone. "This is a very noisy, dirty spot, and I'm sure you will see the man you want just as easily from there. You would find it more comfortable than the taproom," he added. "The types in this part of London can be rough for a gently bred lady."

Sarah agreed with him but did not wish to spend a

moment longer than necessary in his company. Already she was regretting her folly in coming, for any one of the men in the taproom could be the one she was looking for. She would have to tell this wretch a little more in order to help herself. "I have come on behalf of my brother," she admitted reluctantly. "He wishes me to see a man for him, as he is unable to come himself. He is suffering from a slight indisposition, you understand," she lied glibly. "Perhaps you could ask the landlord if a man seeking Mr. Davenant will apply to me."

"But of course. Happy to oblige," Marchmont murmured, releasing her. He moved just inside the door and spoke to an uncouth man in a rough cloth jacket, who nodded. Marchmont returned to her, took her arm again, and led her across to the carriage she had noticed earlier. The horses had now been quieted and put between the shafts. The two beasts stood restlessly pawing the ground. A groom quickly opened the door and helped his master hand Sarah into the vehicle, and Marchmont followed. The steps were pushed up and the door closed.

"Now you may rest comfortably," Marchmont said, leaning back against the blue silk squabs lining the carriage. "Although I say it myself, this is a beautifully sprung chaise, and well worth what I paid for it. Don't you think so?"

"Yes indeed," Sarah agreed. She was looking out of the window anxiously, wondering who it was who had written the note and was expecting to meet her brother. It could be anyone, and her task seemed hopeless.

The uncouth man came out of the tavern and crossed the yard. Sarah put her hand on the door handle. "There is that man you spoke to. He must have found the person I wish to speak to. I must go."

Marchmont raised his hand. Sarah wondered for an instant if he intended to strike her but realized he was signaling to someone instead. "There will be no need for you to leave the carriage," he replied happily. "We are going anyway."

"You might be, but I am certainly not!" Sarah exclaimed in alarm. She tried to open the door but found Marchmont's unexpected strength once more opposing her. "Let go of me," she snapped. "I wish to get out."

"We can conduct your business much more comfortably in here," Marchmont sneered. "You have come in answer to that note, have you not? I believe you did say you were acting on behalf of your brother?"

"Yes, I did say that, and I am," she answered, sitting back again for a moment. "But how do you know about the note?"

The carriage lurched slightly and swung around as the groom maneuvered the frisky team out of the innyard. "I know all about it"—he grinned at her—"because I wrote it. He should have come, but as you are here, you will do very well instead. You are going to take a little journey with me. Relax, my dear. You will be quite safe, I assure you."

Chapter 16

Carton, the butler, was slightly perturbed, a state that was unusual for him. Nuncheon had been ordered for one of the clock and it was now half past, and yet he was assured her ladyship had not returned to the house. He was glad that his master, the marquess, intended to be absent until the dinner hour, for he was very insistent on punctuality. Carton sighed. He decided to ask his lord's sister if she wished the repast served or whether she wanted to wait until Lady Hawkeworth returned.

Lydia was surprised to learn the hour was so advanced. "I have to be back home by three o'clock, so we had better eat now, Carton. Is my brother at home?"

"No, my lady. He is not returning until later," he informed her solemnly.

"My sister is not back yet you say, Carton?" Dominic asked, puzzled by this. It was unlike Sarah to be late.

"So I gather, sir. She is expected," the butler added.

"Oh yes. She told me herself she would be back by now," Lydia put in. "Never mind. Tell them to serve the meal. Lady Hawkeworth will understand, I'm sure."

"Very good," said Carton and retired to give the necessary orders.

"Where did she say she was going?" Dominic asked as soon as the butler disappeared.

"To visit an old servant who lives nearby who is ill," Lydia replied, thinking back to the brief conversation she had had with Sarah earlier in the day. "Now I come to think about it, it is rather strange. I don't know of any servants in Gerry's household who are sick; or if they are they will be abovestairs in the attics and not elsewhere. Could she have gone to see an old retainer of your family?"

Dominic shook his head. "Not that I know of. Only old Nanny lives in London, and she was well when we last saw her. Doesn't live nearby, either. Did Sarah take a carriage?"

"I don't know, but I will find out," Lydia decided.

The servants were unable to help but did say her ladyship had left the house on foot. Not wishing to give rise to unnecessary speculation among the staff, Lydia and Dominic waited until they had finished their meal and were once more alone before discussing Sarah's sudden absence.

"Was she dressed for visiting?" Dominic asked. He kept peering out of the window at every passing coach, expecting his sister to appear.

"It's no good looking at the carriages if she went on foot," Lydia said impatiently. "Stop pacing around, Dominic, and sit down. I think Sarah had on a morning gown, but it was a very plain one. I know," she added, clapping her hands together in relief. "I will go up and ask her maid. She is bound to know where her mistress has gone."

"Is she?"

"Of course, silly. Maids always know everything. You can't keep a secret from a maid!"

Lydia found Annie sorting through drawers of shifts and fine undergarments, but she stopped her work to talk. When asked where her mistress had gone she looked surprised but shook her head regretfully.

"I'm sure I don't know, miss," Annie answered when questioned. "She said nothing to me about going out until this afternoon, when she was taking you home to your mama's. That is why she wanted to wear her old clothes," she added, remembering this item of information.

"She wanted to wear old clothes to take me home?" Lydia queried. "That sounds very odd. Surely you have made a mistake?"

"No indeed, for I asked her plainly why she wanted to wear such an old dress and that was what she said because you had so much luggage and she needed old clothes to help you," Annie repeated stubbornly.

Lydia looked amazed. "We don't deal with the luggage," she said incredulously. "The servants do that. She must have been teasing you. I'm sure she would never visit my mama with an old dress on. Was it really old?"

"Oh yes. The plainest in her wardrobe, and she took her shabbiest cloak, too," Annie informed her. "Oh, miss, do you think something's happened?"

"No, of course not, Annie. Why should it?" Lydia said stoutly.

"Well, Master Dominic was shot at and both of you as well, and then he was kidnapped," Annie insisted. "Maybe Miss Sarah has gone now." She shivered, and began to wring her hands in horror and fright.

"That is nonsense, Annie," Lydia murmured, not very convincingly, for the same thought had gone through her own head only moments before. "But it does seem odd she should go off on foot in old clothes. Did she leave a note behind?"

"No, Miss Lydia. But you expected her back, surely?"

"Yes, we did." Lydia moved restlessly around the bedroom, picking up the brushes from the dressing chest and putting them down again. "I do wonder where she is. Oh, what's that?" she added, noticing a screwed-up piece of paper behind the chest. She bent down and picked it up, smoothing out the crumpled sheet and reading the words written on it.

"The housemaid must have missed it when she cleaned the room. I'll have words to say to her. Too slapdash servants are these days," Annie grumbled with all the assurance of a superior lady's maid. "What is wrong, miss?" she asked as Lydia exclaimed in dismay.

"Oh, nothing Annie, nothing. This note explains the problem, though. I must show it to Dominic. Don't worry about your mistress. I'm sure she will soon be back." Without stopping to answer the startled maid's questions, Lydia rushed off down the stairs and ran into the salon where Dominic had resumed his pacing.

"It is time we left for your mother's," he said heavily. "I wish you were staying here longer, Lydia."

"Oh, never mind that now," she cried, thrusting the paper at him. "Read that, Dominic, and you will see where Sarah has gone. Go on, read it," she said impatiently.

He took the paper and read his own name on the front. "Why, it's addressed to me," he said in surprise.

"Read it."

"Well, all right. Just give me a moment." He turned the note over and read the contents carefully with a growing expression of incredulity on his face, then he read the words again to make sure he was not mistaken. "This is nonsense," he cried. "I don't owe any man five hundred pounds. What absolute rubbish. As if I would leave a debt of honour unpaid for two weeks! Why, it's an insult!"

"But Sarah wouldn't know that. She must have gone to pay it for you," Lydia cried in excitement. "We must follow her."

"Why didn't she give this to me?" Dominic objected crossly. "I would have told her I didn't owe the feller any money. Damned cheek, I call it. Now I suppose she has gone and wasted her blunt for nothing." He smacked his fist into his palm in annoyance.

"If she had gone and paid the money, she would be back by now. It must have been a trick. She has been kidnapped," Lydia was dancing up and down in excitement. "Oh, do stop just standing there and let's go and find her."

"Kidnapped? Do you think so?" he asked. "No. That is nonsense. After all, this was addressed to me, so why kidnap Sarah?"

"If you had received that letter would you have gone to this tavern place—the Swan with Two Necks?" Lydia asked.

"Certainly I would, just to give the feller a piece of my mind. Fancy threatening me! Call him out if he was a gentleman," Dominic said in righteous indignation.

"That's just what I mean. You would have gone and then you would have been kidnapped, as you were at Ranelagh Gardens. Don't you see? It must all be part of a plot."

"I think you read too many novels," Dominic replied testily. "That's a lot of rubbish. I have no enemies, and nor has Sarah. Nobody would kidnap a marchioness."

"They might if they wanted money," Lydia argued.

"They might in that case," he conceded. "But this was addressed to me, and I have no money—at least not much—so your theory is all wrong. I expect Sarah has got there and found she cannot get back again. Might even have got herself lost," he added. "I will go and see if the carriage has been brought around yet. I ordered it to take you home so we can go and find Sarah first and then take you to your mama's."

"Oh, good. I was afraid you would insist on taking me home first. I'll get my cloak."

Lydia sped off, and in a very few minutes both of them were seated in the carriage, and Edward, who had now reverted to his former position as Dominic's groom, was driving them into the city. They found the Swan with Two Necks without any difficulty but no trace of Sarah. She was not in the tavern itself, and the

153

tapster did not remember serving any young lady such as Dominic described, nor did he believe such a person had stepped inside the inn that day.

Dominic returned to the carriage and an impatient Lydia with nothing to report, but just then Edward appeared from the direction of the stables.

"Master Dominic, I found a groom who remembers Miss Sarah," he said in excitement, forgetting to refer to her properly. "She did come here this morning but left again in a fine carriage."

"On her own?"

"No. With a gentleman," Edward explained. "A very fine gentleman with a fancy wig and silk clothes who held a handkerchief to his nose all the time. The groom didn't know his name, but he heard the ostler say they were bound for Buckinghamshire—beyond Uxbridge, I believe."

"Uxbridge? Why, then it must have been Marchmont. He has estates over there. Damn it all, what did Sarah go off with him for?" Dominic cried.

"If he was holding a handkerchief to his nose it must have been Marchmont," Lydia put in. "He is the only man in London who is so affected. Oh, do let's go after them. Do you think he is abducting her?"

"Why would he want to do that?" Dominic was puzzled. "I don't like the feller, but he is my cousin. What can Sarah have been doing?"

"Hmm," Edward said, trying to gain their attention. "I did hear she was not very willing to go. Groom seemed to think she was trying to get out of the carriage as it left the yard but was prevented."

"Was she indeed? That settles it. We will be after them then," Dominic shouted. "Come on, Edward. How much start have they got on us?"

"About two hours, sir."

"Then let 'em go, Edward. We can catch up before dark with a bit of luck."

* * *

The marquess was returning home about an hour later and bumped into his old friend Sir Peter Trevenning in St. James's street.

"Hallo, Gerry. Surprised to see you here," Sir Peter drawled as the marquess was about to step into his carriage. "Thought you must be in the country."

"Why?" Hawkeworth said in some curiosity. "I didn't think I had expressed a wish to rusticate recently. Why did you imagine I had left the delights of the city?"

Sir Peter shrugged his broad shoulders. "Probably because I passed your sister on the road and thought if she was driving out of town you and your lady wife must be in the country as well."

"You saw my sister?" The marquess frowned. "I take it you mean Lydia?"

"Of course. Come in and have a drink with me," Sir Peter invited.

"No. I thank you. Not now. Tell me, please, where did you see my sister and in whose company?"

There was no doubt now about the frown on the marquess's handsome face, and Sir Peter sighed. He had clearly been tactless, and he wished he had not spoken at all. "Perhaps I was mistaken," he suggested hopefully. "Could have been somebody else."

"Where did you see her, Peter?" the marquess replied silkily. "Tell me now and don't prevaricate or I might just lose my temper."

"Not with me you won't. Oh well, don't be too annoyed with her. She is just high-spirited, you know."

"I know my own sister, yes, Peter. Go on. You were telling me where you saw her and whom she was with." The marquess tapped his cane in his gloved hand, and his eyes glinted dangerously.

"I was driving back from Beaconfield and I passed them in a carriage just pulling through Acton village. I suppose they were about to go across the common."

"They?"

"Oh, your wife's brother, Davenant, was with her,"

Sir Peter added, hoping this would not annoy his friend further. He noticed that the information made the marquess draw in his breath and his lips set in a grim line. "They could be out for the day," Sir Peter suggested.

"At four in the afternoon. Hardly. Lydia was returning to my mother's at three," the marquess muttered. Then he remembered he was not alone. "I'll ask you to forget what you saw, Peter," he said sharply. With a brief salute in farewell the marquess jumped into his carriage and ordered the groom to take him to his mother's house as quickly as possible.

There he soon discovered from the butler at the door that his sister had not returned as expected. He swallowed his anger and smiled instead, saying she was staying with him for a little longer. It took him nearly twenty minutes to explain the same excuse to his mother and give a slight indisposition as the reason least likely to upset her. "But she is much better and should be able to come back next week," he reassured her briskly.

"Oh, the poor girl. I must come back with you and see her," the dowager murmured. "She is my baby, you know."

Restraining his temper with an effort, the marquess placated her and managed to prevent her from making any sudden and disastrous visit to his house. He succeeded in getting away himself only by promising to return next day with more news and on the plea of an urgent engagement. From there he went straight to his own house in Grosvenor Square to find his sister missing and his wife as well as her brother. He had expected to confront Sarah and had planned many biting and sarcastic comments to make on the effrontery of her family and the insult in a Davenant eloping with a Hawkeworth, but he was frustrated.

After a few words with Carton he became less annoyed and more worried, particularly on being shown a crumpled note that had been discovered on the floor of the small salon which explained a certain amount but not all. Another note had been handed in for Dominic, which the marquess scanned quickly under the affronted eyes of the butler. He came to a swift decision but took care to take the papers with him.

After a quick change of clothes he left the house behind a fresh team of horses with only a groom for company. He wasted no time in going to the city but set his horses westward, where he was sure he would find the answer to the puzzle.

Chapter 17

Lydia had been far too excited when they set out from the Swan with Two Necks to think of dinner or indeed of anything so mundane as food. Yet when six o'clock had passed and they were still driving she began to feel hunger pangs and wonder if they could stop. Dominic at first dismissed her pleas, for he was too anxious to catch up with his cousin and his sister to worry about refreshments, but when Uxbridge came in sight he, too, felt that they could afford to stop for a short rest to change the horses and enjoy a quick bite to eat.

"But it must be quick, mind," he added, as Lydia thankfully climbed down from the carriage. "I think we have made sufficiently good time to be close on their heels, and if I am right, Marchmont's estate is no more than ten miles or so from here, not far from Tatling End."

"What a peculiar name for a place," Lydia said, tripping ahead of him into the inn. "Do you think we can obtain a private parlor? I would like to sit down for a while in peace after that drive."

"I'll see," Dominic agreed and was soon in conversation with the landlord.

Mine host decided that these visitors were quality

and deserved the best. He ruthlessly overruled the prior claim of a traveling merchant and his wife, and in no time Lydia was installed in a snug parlor waiting for her dinner to be brought up. Dominic was less happy to be reclining at ease and felt he should have insisted on a quick change of horses so that they could press on to their destination.

"But why need we hurry now, Dominic?" Lydia asked him. "It is too late for us to return to London this evening, so Lord Marchmont will be forced to offer us a bed for the night. If we catch up with Sarah in one hour or two it makes little difference."

Dominic could see the logic in this argument, but he was still disturbed. "We don't know what he plans to do with her," he complained. "We could be too late."

"Too late for what? Surely you don't think he plans to harm her, do you?"

"No," Dominic admitted reluctantly. "But I can't work out what he does intend to do. It all seems so pointless to me."

"Maybe he just wanted to show her his estate."

"Then why not ask her to go properly? No, there must be something else behind it. After all, he wanted me in the first place."

"So he did. I had forgotten that," murmured the volatile Lydia. "We could be walking into a trap if he wants you as well. How exciting!"

"Certainly not. There is nothing exciting about a chase like this. Still, you could be right and I must not expose you to any danger. I think I should ask the landlord to prepare a room for you and you can spend the night here in safety. That would be the best plan."

"Oh, you cannot do anything so mean!" Lydia exclaimed. "Why, I must come with you. I refuse to be left here alone."

"I knew we should have brought your maid along," Dominic was objecting when the door opened to admit the landlord. He was followed by two maids carrying dishes. In a trice the covers were laid and a delicious aroma made both of them forget their argument.

Lydia did hearty justice to the broiled pigeons with artichoke bottoms, breast of veal with green peas, a marrow pudding, and Scotch collops. She followed these with a large dish of almond flummery, some orange pudding, and assorted fruit tarts. Dominic had managed a little of the pigeons and veal, but since he was more concerned about his sister's welfare he resisted the flummery and absently picked at a bowl of fresh cherries.

"I think I should set out now," he said after a few moments. He pushed back his plate and got up from the table.

Lydia spat out a cherrystone she had nearly swallowed. "Then I am coming too," she announced. "You cannot leave me behind. If you do I shall hire a chaise and follow you," she added with spirit.

"I can't bear to think of you running into danger," Dominic said anxiously. "It is bad enough that my sister is in the hands of this man, but if he got you too . . ." His voice trailed off, and Lydia flung herself into his arms.

"I'm sorry, Dom. I didn't mean to upset you, but I do so want to come with you. Don't leave me alone here."

"Very affecting," drawled a voice sharply from the doorway. Both young people spun around in horror, for they had not heard the door opening. Lydia gasped in dismay when she saw her brother, and Dominic turned red, then rather white as he realized the compromising position he appeared to be in.

"It's not what you are thinking," he stuttered unhappily.

"We are chasing Sarah to get her back for you," Lydia interrupted eagerly, now her first fright was over.

"Are you indeed," the marquess said sarcastically. "Well, I am relieved to find you are not eloping, anyway."

"Eloping?" Lydia was shocked into a giggle. "I never thought of that."

"Certainly not," Dominic said stiffly.

The marquess raised his eyebrows and looked from one to the other, making Dominic feel like a naughty schoolboy. Lydia was unconcerned and returned to the table to pick up a few more cherries. She knew her brother better. "Oh, do come in and tell us why you are here, Gerry," she said happily. "Now I know you will let me go with you, for it would be improper to leave me here without a maid, and I cannot take harm with my brother."

"I certainly require explanations from you both, but I am relieved to find my suspicions are apparently unfounded," Hawkeworth said. He closed the door firmly on an interested servitor. "Did you stop to think about poor Mama?" he added, turning to his sister and ignoring Dominic, who shuffled his feet nervously.

Lydia put a hand to her mouth in consternation. "Oh dear! I forgot that I was expected home by three o'clock," she said aghast. "Oh, what will she say?"

"Nothing, for I went around to put her mind at rest," her brother assured her. "You are at present recovering from a slight indisposition and unable to see any visitors. You will return home when you are fit again. I think that covers the situation well enough."

Lydia ran across and clasped his hand. "You know, you really are not half as bad as people think but the kindest of brothers," she said warmly.

"Spare me such praise, Lydia, before you overwhelm me. Instead, tell me, Dominic, what this chase is in aid of and where your sister is at this moment," he asked peremptorily.

Dominic was only too glad to disclose the whole sequence of events. He was relieved to find the marquess did not intend to tear him off a strip for his rash conduct in bringing Lydia out of town, and it occurred to him that as her husband the marquess stood in a far better position when it came to rescuing Sarah or at least discovering what was going on in Lord Marchmont's house. He outlined all he knew and what he and Lydia had discovered at the Swan with Two Necks in Lad Lane. He finished his story and waited hopefully to see what his brother-in-law would say.

"I think we should set out for Marchmont's estates now," he suggested tentatively after a few moments' silence.

The marquess continued his musing, then looked up. "I am tempted to leave you both here and go on by myself," he said thoughtfully. "I think I can handle him alone."

"Oh, that would be infamous, Gerry! I will not stay here." Lydia stamped her foot.

"I intend to rescue my sister myself," Dominic snapped and glared at the marquess, his uncomfortable situation forgotten for the present.

"I think that neither of you is in a position to query my decisions," the marquess said calmly. "However, you might be useful, Dominic."

"And what about me?" Lydia's indignation burst forth. "If Sarah is in any trouble she will need a female to assist her, or had you forgotten that?" She regarded her brother in triumph.

"No. I had not discounted that, so I will take you as well," the marquess conceded. "How much do you know of the place itself, Dominic? I confess I have never been there. Is it a sizable house? And I wonder if he employs many servants?"

"The main house is a large one, and there is a shooting lodge at the other end of the estate," Dominic volunteered. "I visited there when I was twelve and can give you a fair idea of the layout. But as to servants, who can tell if he employs many there? He has owned the estate for only a few months, so some of the old retainers might still be employed."

"Good. That sounds promising," Hawkeworth commented. He listened carefully while Dominic told him what he could remember.

"What is all this about, Gerry?" Lydia asked, impatient to join in the conversation once more. "I wish you would explain if you know. Clearly Dominic should have been captured instead of Sarah, but why does Marchmont want either of them?"

"Yes. It beats me," Dominic admitted. "Do you know, my lord?"

"Oh, I have a very fair notion of what it is all about," the marquess told them. "But there is no need to go into details now. We must set off before darkness falls. At all events, it's a fine evening, which will be in our favor. Now I'll go down and settle your shot with the landlord while you get yourselves ready. We had better take both carriages, as mine is my racing curricle and will carry only my groom and myself. We might need that man of yours, Edward, too," he added as he left the room.

Only minutes later, Dominic and Lydia were down in the innyard prepared to set out. Dominic helped Lydia into the carriage and told Edward to follow the marquess's vehicle and keep as close as he could.

Lydia snuggled up to Dominic and sighed. "I wonder what is happening to Sarah," she murmured. "I do hope she is in no danger."

Chapter 18

Sarah herself had been more indignant than frightened when the carriage first set off from the Swan with Two Necks. After struggling to get out of the door as the vehicle began to move and finding Lord Marchmont too strong for her, she gave up and sat back opposite him, glowering out of the window at the passing traffic. It occurred to her that the carriage was traveling along the same road taken by the hackney which had brought her into the city. She decided it might be possible to open the window and call for help when they neared the neighborhood where she had been living.

Lord Marchmont must have guessed her thoughts. "I don't advise you to do anything reckless," he said softly. "Nobody will listen to shrieks coming from a carriage, and certainly no one is likely to aid you in any way. On the other hand, I should be very annoyed indeed if you cause such a disturbance and would take steps to see you do not do so again." To illustrate his point he picked up a long ebony cane with a curiously wrought silver handle. In an instant the fascinated Sarah watched as a thin blade hissed out and the stick was transformed into a deadly rapier. He waved it nonchalantly in the air, but his sharp eyes studied her face, and she gathered his meaning quite plainly.

"There is no need to threaten me," she snapped at him, still too ruffled to be really frightened. "I have no intention of risking my life dangling out of a coach window."

"I'm very glad to hear it," he replied smoothly and thrust the sword back into the case. The now harmless cane was placed beside him on the seat, but Sarah noticed his delicate white hand stayed very close to it.

"Why have you taken me up in your carriage?" she demanded after gazing out of the window for some time. They were now traveling along Tyburn Road and approaching the infamous tree. She shuddered and averted her eyes at the sight of a corpse dangling there and found Lord Marchmont laughing at her.

"I have brought you with me because I had little choice in the matter. If you are not happy about it then you have only yourself to blame for meddling in my affairs," he told her. "You should have given my letter to your brother and you would not have been involved at all."

"What did you want with him?" she asked curiously. "You have little in common."

He tittered. "There you are certainly correct, my dear. I abhor healthy, sporting young gentlemen like your brother. I believe he went to a prizefight only the other day. Ugh!" The scent of musk was wafted from his handkerchief as he buried his nose in the folds once more.

"That is not the point at all," said Sarah impatiently. "I want to know why you wished to meet him at that tavern. He did not owe you any money, I'm certain, so why did you talk about a debt of honour? It was all nonsense."

He nodded his head. "Most of it was, yes, my dear. But I did wish to speak to him, and if I had written under my own name he would not have come. So I invented a debt and accused him of it, knowing he would come to the meeting just to see who was insulting him so. It is quite simple."

Sarah could agree with his reasoning thus far, but she could not guess what was behind it all. "You have not told me why you wished to speak to him," she pointed out.

"No, I have not, have I? Stupid of me. I am not used to curious females, you see, so you will have to be patient."

Sarah decided he was prevaricating and wondered if she could get the truth out of him another way. "What do you intend to do with me?" she asked innocently. "Are you taking me to your house in Buckinghamshire?"

"I am." His tone was noncommittal. "As you have been there before in your youth, you may remember it. I hope that when your brother receives my second note he will come after you."

"You mean you still want to see him?"

"Oh, indeed I do. It is imperative that he come. It would all have been so much more convenient in London and without you around to confuse the issue, but I must make the best of the present circumstances." He sighed petulantly.

"I wish you would not talk in such riddles." Sarah had lost her patience and was growing irritated by this pampered man who sat opposite her studying his nails. "You want to see my brother and you are now using me as a bait to draw him into the country. Is that correct?"

"It is indeed. How clever you are," he congratulated her.

"You have still not told me why."

"I suppose I must do so. I had intended your brother to meet with a fatal accident not far from that tavern. It was all arranged," he added as she gasped at his words. "There is so much violence in London these days that another death would have surprised nobody and caused little concern. However, I have had to rethink my plans. A pity." He relapsed into silence again and brought out a small buffer, with which he polished his nails carefully.

For a short while Sarah was too overcome to say anything further. She was not usually rendered speechless, but the man's casual way of talking about killing another human being, and that one her brother, was so cold-blooded. She shivered involuntarily, and he looked up and smiled at her.

"You need have no fear for your own safety," he assured her. "I wish you no harm at all, and if you remain sensible you will be able to return to your home and your husband in a few days. That is, if he still wants you," he added with a mirthless laugh.

"Why shouldn't he?" she said without thinking.

"Oh, I'm sure you know the answer to that without my telling you. The beautiful Miss Masterson is irresistible, but soon she will be my wife, and he will have to look elsewhere for his amours."

Sarah wanted to slap his face and shout at him that he was a liar and her husband had no amours, but remembering the night at Ranelagh she could not do so, and the countless occasions when her husband had left her side at parties and balls. This man was intending to be cruel but she knew the truth of his taunts and stayed silent to recover her composure. She then recalled his former plans for her brother and dared to ask him what would happen to Dominic when he followed them into the country.

"It is better that you do not know anything at all about the matter," he told her curtly. "He will suffer an accident, that is all. The details are unimportant."

"To you, maybe, but not to him," she snapped. "Why do you wish him dead?"

"Let us just say I dislike the young man and all he stands for. He has insulted me and will pay for it," Marchmont said coldly.

Sarah sat back, and as the miles passed she considered Marchmont's words. There was something wrong in what he had said. She knew him to be arrogant and foppish, but he did not seem the sort of man to risk a charge of murder just because he had been insulted. There must be more behind it than that. She racked her brains to think what it could be. "You must have organized his abduction from Ranelagh," she said as realization came to her.

"I did indeed, but my hireling bungled the job. He was supposed to kill your brother, not merely knock him senseless so that the Watch would find him. The fool went back to finish the job at my orders but found Davenant spirited away to the Roundhouse." Marchmont looked bitter.

"Did more of your hirelings shoot at us that day on our return from Knightsbridge?" she asked.

He nodded. "Again, more bungling fools. This time I decided I must deal with the job and complete it properly."

"If you let me go, I can tell the world how you planned my brother's death," Sarah said recklessly. "You should have chosen to fight a duel, not to murder him in this underhand way."

"I think you will be silent if you know what's good for you," Marchmont retorted quietly. "What I have done to your brother I can do to you just as easily. Cutthroats can be hired very cheaply from the stews and the waterside. Don't forget that, my dear, and you will keep your pretty tongue silent."

"My husband will believe me," she said foolishly.

"Do you think so?" he inquired, lifting his eyebrows in surprise. "Remember, I know the truth about your marriage. I was present at the time of the infamous bet, and although Hawkeworth silenced the rumors quickly, he cannot deceive me, and knows it. I think he will prefer to forget anything you tell him for the sake of keeping his family name unsullied. His reputation means a great deal to him, and you, I think, do not," he added viciously.

Unable to answer such a telling argument, Sarah sank back and tried to stop her thoughts from racing ahead to the trap planned for Dominic. How could she warn him? If she could get free at the house, maybe she would have an opportunity to escape and intercept him before he arrived. The chance was a slender one, but she decided to attempt to rest in order to save her strength. Her companion ignored her as she curled up in the corner, but it was impossible to stop herself from thinking about all she had just been told. The coach jogged on and the miles between herself and anyone who could help her stretched out longer and longer.

When at last the coach turned into a rutted drive she was bounced into awareness that the end of the journey was in sight. She sat up and watched Lord Marchmont warily. Dusk was falling, and it was difficult to read his expression. Maybe she would have a chance to get away when the coach stopped, but a moment later she knew that was a vain hope. Marchmont took hold of his sword stick and unsheathed the blade.

"Just to remind you to be sensible," he murmured. "I am adept at the art."

The coach stopped, and a groom appeared at the window.

"Your servants will be surprised to see you escorting me at swordpoint," she challenged him. "I might even remember some of them. It is only eight years since I visited here."

"My aunt's servants have all been dismissed or retired," he replied at once. "And my men have more sense than to question their master."

Sarah said nothing more but got out of the coach and allowed herself to be escorted across the gravel drive toward the front door of the sprawling Tudor mansion. She could remember the warm red brick she had liked all those years ago, but in the dusk with only one lighted window it looked gloomy and uninviting. As she trod up the steps with Lord Marchmont close behind she wondered why he had dismissed her great-aunt's servants. Faithful retainers were hard to come by. Did he have a more sinister reason?

She had reached the hall and begun to cross it before the truth struck her. She stopped so suddenly Lord Marchmont almost bumped into her, and she heard his exclamation of annoyance. She turned around to him in triumph. "I know why you want to be rid of Dominic," she said clearly. "You have no right to be here at all. He should have inherited all this and not you. How did you manage to convince everyone of your right to the estate?"

He paused and looked at her. "You fool! You stupid little fool." He swore at her softly. "Now you, too, must be disposed of. I think poor Hawkeworth got his just deserts after all in marrying you. What could be worse than a plain woman but a clever one! Come." He grabbed her arm roughly, and a man standing in the shadows thrust open a door.

Sarah found herself in a small chamber lit by one large candelabra that threw shadows on the shrouded furniture.

With an oath, Marchmont whipped the covers off two chairs and thrust the girl into one of them. He then turned and gave rapid orders to the servant still standing by the door. The man turned around and disappeared, but Marchmont came to stand beside her chair. "You have been just too clever for your own good. If you had not guessed the answer, you could have gone back to Hawkeworth as I told you and he would have said nothing. Now I must find some way of disposing of you both."

"Another accident?" she suggested.

He glanced at her. "And why not? Who will miss you, after all? I might acquire a rival for Miss Masterson's favors once more, but that is preferable to losing all this." His arm swept around to encompass the room and the house. "Oh no. I don't intend to lose everything now I have got hold of it."

"How did you manage it?" she asked. "You still haven't told me. Are you an impostor?"

"That is not your business. You have discovered enough. Now I intend to leave you upstairs while I make my preparations. You will be quite safe in the old nurseries, and there is no way you can escape, so don't try, my dear. You will merely cause me great inconvenience and hurt yourself. Wait until your brother arrives. You can commit suicide together." He tittered, but Sarah did not appreciate the joke.

Marchmont opened the door and beckoned to the servant. "Take her to the nurseries and lock her in," he commanded abruptly. "Make sure she cannot get out."

The man nodded, and Sarah found herself being led roughly up two flights of stairs to the nurseries she remembered dimly from that past visit. Then she and her brother had enjoyed playing in the rooms, but now, in the dark, they were musty, damp, and offered little hope of escape.

Once she was left alone she did her best to explore the two rooms, which were linked by a connecting door. She could make out the few items of furniture in the moonlight now coming through the uncurtained windows. These were her first hope, but the rusty bars across them precluded escape that way. The door had been firmly locked, and she found that the door of the connecting room was also locked. There seemed little hope of getting out before Lord Marchmont decided to release her to join Dominic and suffer that fatal accident. She stood wretchedly in the middle of the room, wishing she had not interfered. Her brother might have saved himself as he had done on the previous occasions, but now she was involved he would have no chance, for he would never sacrifice her as well.

She crossed to the window and looked out. So close she could almost touch it was the branch of a large elm tree, but the bars stood between her and freedom. In fury she grabbed at them and shook them fiercely. The next moment she was stumbling back into the room with the bars in her hand. They had been in the wood for so long that a combination of rot and rust had loosened them and they had come free when she tugged. It was the work of a moment to prise two more out, although her hands were scraped in the process. She then pushed her head out through the space and studied the tree intently. If she pulled out another bar she could just squeeze through the gap and reach the branch. Whether or not it would bear her weight was a risk she would have to take.

The idea had no sooner come than she struggled to carry it out, but the last bar resisted her efforts. Pushing, pulling, and tugging seemed useless, until at last it broke free and she fell to the floor still holding the metal in her hand. The thought of the drop below her was almost unnerving, but then if she stayed she would probably die some other way, so there was little choice.

Her skirts would hamper her descent, so Sarah tugged off her small hoop and the petticoats underneath her gown, leaving only her dress, which she hitched up to free her legs. She climbed out through the gap and launched herself into the tree. The branch cracked and swayed violently but did not break. She slithered along it to the comparative safety of the trunk and clung there for a moment to still her thumping heart. It took longer than she had expected to climb down, and several times she was certain she would fall before she slipped the last few feet to land in the grass.

She stole around the outside of the house searching for the front drive. Dominic would come this way, she was sure, and keeping this in mind she moved around the gravel sweep, keeping to the shelter of the overgrown shrubbery. Halfway down she felt safe enough to move onto the drive itself, and then she began to run toward the gates.

In the distance she heard the sound of wheels and paused for a moment, terrified she was being chased by Marchmont already. Then she realized the sound came from a vehicle on the road ahead, and it was probably her brother coming to confront Marchmont. Without any thought for her safety, she rushed out of the gates almost into the path of an oncoming chaise.

Chapter 19

With an oath the marquess saw the figure rushing toward him and pulled on the horses' heads, swinging the curricle sideways to avoid a collision. By his skilled horsemanship he managed to avert a disaster, but he noticed the person fall to the ground as he wrestled to control his team. Flinging the reins aside and shouting to the groom to hold their heads, he sprang down and ran to the heap lying in the grass by the roadside.

He realized it was a woman, and as she struggled to sit up he recognized her. "Sarah!" he exclaimed. "Are you all right?"

"I think so," she murmured. "I tripped. I thought you would run me down."

"I nearly did so. What a stupid thing to do, rushing out in front of a carriage," he said, his relief making him speak more sharply than he intended. He picked her up in his arms and strode toward his coach just as Dominic's vehicle came to a stop a few yards away.

Sarah was so relieved to see her husband that she forgot his harsh words and clung to him, hardly able to believe the terror of the last few hours was at an end.

"What has happened?" Dominic cried. He jumped

down and came up to join them. "Why have you stopped? Did you run someone down?"

"It's Sarah. She rushed out of the gates almost under my horses' hooves," the marquess explained. "I think she has taken no hurt."

"I am unharmed, just bruised," she reassured them both as her husband helped her to sit down on the curricle's seat. "But you must not go up to the house, Dominic, for Lord Marchmont plans your death in some accident."

"Does he indeed! I'll soon see about that. Marchmont is mad!" Dominic said roundly. "Fancy taking you off like this. Did he let you go?"

"Tell us all that has happened to you, quickly," the marquess put in urgently.

"And me," cried another voice indignantly. Lydia came rushing up, having scrambled out of Dominic's carriage unaided and run along the road to see what was going on. "Oh, Sarah, it is you. I am so pleased to see you. Now we won't have to rescue you after all."

"Were you coming to rescue me?" Sarah asked, looking bewildered when she saw how many people there were. "Lord Marchmont said he had left another note for Dominic to lure him here, but he said you would not be bothered, sir," she added, turning to the marquess.

"Just tell us all you know and then I will deal with him," the marquess said grimly. "I have several scores to settle with him now."

Sarah was pleased at this attitude, although she could not understand the change of heart. However, she had to warn them that they must on no account go on into danger. She explained all that had happened to her and chiefly what had been said in her conversations with Marchmont. "So you see, he is likely to kill you both, and us too if he can," she finished.

"Has he many servants in the place?" the marquess asked, ignoring the warning.

Sarah wrinkled her brow in thought. "I only saw one

man who took me up to the nurseries, but Marchmont had two grooms with him on the way down and must have had other servants in the house, although it looked very deserted and the furniture was still under holland covers."

"Good." Her husband sounded pleased, but she could not see his expression in the dark. "I doubt if he has many men with him, and none to match us. Now Sarah, you and my sister will stay in Dominic's chaise with Edward, while Dominic and I go into the house and settle our differences."

"He will kill you," Sarah said in distress. "He is determined not to lose his estates, and now he knows we are aware of the truth he will have to silence you."

"He can try but will never succeed," the marquess said confidently. "Don't worry. Lydia, go back to the other carriage. I will bring Sarah. And you, Edward, will stay in the driving seat, and if you hear anything untoward you will drive the ladies back to Uxbridge at once. Do you understand?"

"Yes, my lord," Edward murmured, sounding awed and impressed. He had been, with the marquess's own groom, a silent spectator, and had taken in the whole story eagerly. Now it was clear he would prefer to join in the excitement but was resigned to his place in charge of the ladies.

The marquess lifted his wife once more and strode over to the other coach with her. She found being in his arms very pleasant and wished she could stay there, but in another moment she would be left in the coach and he would be risking his life. "Be careful," she whispered anxiously. "Please be careful, sir."

"Have no fears for me. Marchmont will suffer, not I, for daring to abduct my wife," he murmured, placed her in the coach, and he was gone.

As the carriage rolled slowly up the drive behind the marquess's curricle, Sarah felt a warm glow inside her. In spite of all Marchmont had said, her husband had come to her aid, and even if he was concerned only with his family name, still he had come.

The house still showed only a couple of lights as both coaches came to a stop near the door. Edward remained in his seat, ready to set off again if necessary, while the other groom stood holding the horses' heads and the two men strode to the door. After pounding loudly, they were admitted, and the two ladies were forced to wait outside not knowing what was happening.

Dominic found himself growing excited; the palms of his hands were damp and he longed to get his hands on the man who had not only stolen his sister but, it seemed, had taken his inheritance as well. However, he had promised his brother-in-law to remain silent and leave the talking to him unless it proved necessary for either of them to resort to violence.

The marquess, totally in command and apparently unruffled, followed the rather rough footman who had opened the door. He demanded to be shown into Lord Marchmont's presence at once, and the servitor did so unaware that this was not the man his master expected.

Marchmont was sitting in the room where he had first taken Sarah. The furniture had been uncovered and a small fire lit in spite of the June heat to take the damp chill off the place. He jumped to his feet on seeing his visitors, and his mouth dropped open in complete surprise. "You!" he stuttered at last. "Why are you here?"

"Oh, I think you know the answer to that," Hawkeworth murmured. "Now, send your man off and we can talk in private. We have much to discuss."

"Have we?" said Lord Marchmont, who was clearly trying to gather his scattered wits and adjust to this new situation. "I am not sure I wish to be left with two such desperate gentlemen as you are. Hodgeson can stay." The man nodded and took up his position by the door.

"If you wish our business to be the subject of low

tavern gossip in every hole in London, by all means let him stay," the marquess replied. "I think you would do better to send him upstairs to check on the nurseries. That is where you locked my wife, I believe."

"How do you know?" Marchmont snapped in alarm. "How could you possibly know that? You fool!" he shouted, rounding on the servant. "Didn't you lock both doors?"

"Oh, he locked them, but you did not calculate on the strength of character shown by a member of the Davenant family, particularly when faced with her own and her brother's possible death," Hawkeworth continued before the man could reply. "She is now safely in my carriage with my sister, so her reputation remains unsullied, an important point when dealing with scum like you. My grooms are ready to defend them, so there is little you can do to harm her further."

Marchmont was breathing hard, but his eyes were still cold and watchful. He waved the man from the room, and when the three of them were alone some of his confidence returned. "You may have your wife back, although I don't know how, but I still have the two of you. If I so desire you would both be dead before you could return to your coaches and your grooms."

The marquess shrugged. He moved across and poured himself a glass of wine from the tray of decanters standing on a table. Both Dominic and Marchmont seemed somewhat unnerved by his calm demeanor. When he had a full glass the marquess resumed the conversation. "You may not be a gentleman, but you have some intelligence, I believe. Our deaths would do you no good at all and would take a great deal of explaining in polite circles."

"Your death might, but his would not," Marchmont said, pointing to Dominic, who glowered back. "His death would set me completely free." He reached behind him in the chair and pulled out a tiny pistol, aiming straight for Dominic's heart. Before he could pull the trigger he received the glass of wine full in the face, and the shot went wide, glancing off the ceiling cornice harmlessly.

"Perhaps I have credited you with more intelligence than you do possess," the marquess said, reaching over and removing the pistol, which he dropped into his own pocket. "Your life of ease is coming to an end now."

"Never," Marchmont bellowed in his reedy voice. "My God, I could kill you with my bare hands for this." Wine was pouring over his face, coat, and lace cravat. "My clothes are ruined, damn you, ruined!"

"There speaks the eternal valet," the marquess drawled in amusement. "Mark him well, Dominic. Clothes have been his life."

"I don't understand all this. Stop talking about clothes and let's teach the feller a lesson," Dominic interrupted impatiently.

"All in good time. See how white he has gone." Hawkeworth lounged on the table swinging a leg casually. "He knows I can unmask him completely, and whatever his threats he cannot dispose of me. I took the precaution of informing my lawyers of the whole affair. They will be acting for the new heir—you, Dominic—as soon as they are in possession of all the relevant documents."

"I've burned them," Marchmont murmured sullenly. He had relapsed back into the chair, the wine stains forgotten. His face was now very pale, and the glance of hatred he directed against the marquess told everything.

"Your master is dead, is he not?" Hawkeworth continued, changing the subject slightly. "It was a clever idea to take his place, and if his aunt had been without other living relatives as you thought, you would have been safe."

"So my great-aunt, did have a relative, then. He is her cousin," Dominic put in.

"Oh no. Not cousin, but nephew, and it is not this man who was related to Lady Marchmont but his master.

When she died, the shock was so great that his master, too, had a heart attack and passed away. This evil fellow saw his opportunity for obtaining riches and an easy life and stepped into his shoes. His master was a dandy, and what better disguise could you have than the wigs, paint, and patches the foppish fraternity go in for? As his late master's valet this man was in an excellent position to imitate him and even to show grief at the sudden demise of his servant. He played his part so well that society accepted him, and he might have got away with the deception but for you and your sister."

"Our arrival in town was inopportune," Dominic agreed. "But we would never have suspected. I believed him, and so did Sarah."

"You did, but he could not feel easy with a real relative so close at hand, and one moreover who should be the true heir. My marriage to your sister gave you both even greater prominence. He encouraged you to gamble so that you would be deeply in debt and forced to leave London or even to become beholden to him, but that failed. Then he tried several clumsy attempts to dispatch you before deciding to deal with the matter in person, and so we reach this present outrage. A stupid move by a weak man. He has overreached himself."

"You can never prove all that," Marchmont said suddenly. He sat up again, and a crafty look came into his eyes. "It will be my word against yours, and my standing in society is as high as yours."

"Do you think so? You amaze me," Hawkeworth murmured. "I am not sure if I should spike you through for that insult, but since you are not a gentleman I can offer you no challenge." He sounded regretful.

"Remember I know all the details of your hasty marriage. Such a scandal will be greatly appreciated in London," Marchmont went on. "You cannot prove anything against me, and I merely invited your sister, my relative, to visit. Any hysterical outburst she makes to

180

the contrary will sound like the outpourings of a dishonored woman," he sneered.

Dominic went for his sword, but the marquess stopped him. Grim now and without the humor he had kept so far, Hawkeworth looked down at his victim. "You betray your origins with every word," he said softly. "Oh, you could try your slanders, but I think my reputation will take no permanent harm. However, it will not be necessary. I have here a paper stating all the details of your imposture. You will sign it and then take yourself off and disappear. If you show up again I will not be held accountable for your carcass."

"I will not sign anything. You are mad to expect it," Marchmont snapped. "I can outface you. My standing is high."

"Do you think it will survive an exhumation order on your late master? I have already instigated such through my lawyers, and I believe the late Jeremy Danton had several interesting birthmarks which will prove conclusively that you are a lying impostor. Several notable persons knew him. They are living retired in the country, but I have approached them, and when they meet you you will be finished. You have enjoyed another man's wealth and position for some months now, but that is all over. The real heir, my brother-in-law, will inherit everything. He is, after all, Lady Marchmont's great-nephew; his mother was her husband's niece. You can return to wherever you came from. Now sign the paper." He thrust an official-looking piece of paper in front of Marchmont and walked across to pick up a pen from a desk in the corner.

The man sitting slumped in the chair had wilted completely. There was no more fight left in him. He picked up the pen and signed his name—his real name— at the foot of the page where the marquess indicated.

Studying the document closely, the marquess seemed satisfied. When the signature was dry he folded the paper and put it back into the pocket of his coat.

Marchmont got to his feet and stumbled from the room. They heard him run off toward the back of the house, and another door slammed.

Dominic was still standing in much the same position, looking stunned, when Lydia burst into the room, followed closely by Edward and then Sarah.

"What has happened? Where is Lord Marchmont?" she demanded fiercely. "We heard a shot, but Sarah would not let me come in, then we heard sounds from the stables. Has he gone?"

"I imagine so," said the marquess cheerfully, as he finished a fresh glass of wine. "We disposed of him neatly, as you might say. Now you can congratulate the new heir and soon to be created Lord Marchmont."

Lydia looked at Dominic and cried out in delight. "You really are going to inherit all his fortune. Oh, how marvelous. Now Gerry will approve of your suit, for you will have almost as much money as he has."

"Lydia!" Sarah exclaimed, shocked. But she crossed the room and kissed Dominic in some relief.

"You are quite right, little sister, but I deplore the manners you show," the marquess murmured. "Dominic will be welcome to you. I think it might be suitable for you to delay your nuptials for six months or so, though, to enable him to get used to his new status."

"I can't believe it," Dominic admitted. "It sounds just like one of those dreadful novels Sarah used to get from the circulating library."

"I do agree with you," Hawkeworth said. "But perhaps we should return to Uxbridge. I took the precaution of ordering rooms for us all for the night. I think we shall be more comfortable there."

Sarah had drawn nearer to her husband and now took his arm shyly, smiling up at him. "I am so pleased that nothing terrible happened," she whispered. "I was so afraid he would hurt you."

The marquess looked down at her tenderly, but at that moment his sister chose to giggle and remark naughtily, "Now Miss Masterson will have lost both the fortunes she was chasing. Don't you think that's splendid, Sarah?"

Sarah withdrew her arm from her husband at once at the mention of Miss Masterson's name, and he cursed Lydia under his breath. Before he could do anything to correct the situation his own groom burst into the room.

"Oh, my lord, come quickly. There's been an accident. That dandified lord we come to see has been tossed from his horse. Broken his neck, I think. Come quick."

The marquess nodded tersely. "Right. Now, Edward, take the ladies back to Uxbridge in Mr. Davenant's carriage and we will be along later." He turned to Sarah and Lydia. "I am afraid we must stay and sort this matter out. Take the carriage, and retire when you reach the inn. You will be safe enough if you share the same room. I don't know when we will be there, but you will see us tomorrow morning. Go now."

Lydia was about to object, but Sarah took her arm firmly. "Come along, Lydia," she said quietly. "There is nothing we can do to help now."

Chapter 20

Next morning Lydia was awake bright and early, eager to chatter about the exciting events of the day before. Sarah, in spite of being very tired from all she had been through, had not slept very well. She had been troubled by wild dreams in which the figure of Lord Marchmont pursued her husband and wrenched her from his arms, where she was at once replaced by Miss Masterson while Marchmont's laughter echoed round.

It was still hard for both girls to believe that Dominic was about to become Lord Marchmont, although Lydia was bubbling over with joy that her brother had agreed to her betrothal. Sarah had to help the girl to dress, for neither of them had their maids. Sarah herself had little difficulty, for most of her petticoats were on the floor of the nurseries at Tatling End. When they had completed a sketchy toilette, both repaired to the private parlor which had been hired for them with the bedchambers and there found both Dominic and the marquess eating a hearty breakfast.

"Is it true? Is he dead?" Lydia asked at once when the serving maid had left the room.

"Yes. It's quite true. He broke his neck in the fall," the marquess replied. "As this has happened we think it might be as well to forget all that has taken place in the last few days."

"Save scandal," Dominic muttered through a mouthful of ham.

"And we must save scandal at all costs," Sarah put in bitterly.

Her husband's eyebrows rose a fraction, but he made no comment. Instead he continued with what he had been saying before being interrupted. "Dominic is the only legitimate heir, and there will be no objections. So to save dragging the whole story into the open we can just let him inherit as he will do anyway. We have notified the coroner, and the formalities are being attended to."

"What about that inquiry into his master's body which you said you had begun?" Dominic asked, remembering what the marquess had said.

"Oh that. Well, that was only an invention on my part. A wild suggestion to frighten him." Hawkeworth grinned. "I have done nothing of the sort, nor did I know for certain he was an impostor until all this happened. I guessed at part, but the rest was just pure luck."

"You carried it off well anyway," Dominic murmured admiringly. "I believed you."

"So did he, which was the important thing. The paper he signed was very ambiguous too, but I could have written in more afterward if it had been necessary. Now he has saved us the trouble. I think we should return to town," he added, getting to his feet. "My dear mama will be worried about her sick daughter."

Lydia giggled and explained to the puzzled Sarah what excuses her brother had made to explain why she had not returned home as planned. "Gerry is very good at inventing stories, as you can see," Lydia said happily.

"Yes, I know," Sarah said quietly.

The marquess studied her face and took her arm firmly in his. "Now, Lydia, I intend to permit you to

travel with Dominic, but I expect you to behave yourself. To ensure that you do, my groom will ride behind
and Edward in front."

"Oh, why?" she objected at once. "Can't Sarah travel
with us and tell me her adventures?"

Before Sarah could answer, the marquess ruthlessly
crushed this suggestion. "No, she cannot, for she is
going to tell me instead. Now, no arguing if you wish
me to persuade Mama Dominic is a suitable match for
you. Go along now."

Lydia went murmuring about tyrannical brothers,
but she was happy enough to be settled beside Dominic, and they drove off while the marquess's curricle
was still being brought around.

"Now maybe we can enjoy a little peace from Lydia's
chatter," he remarked as they set off. "I think we have
one or two matters to discuss between us."

"Do we?" she countered.

"We do. Why, for instance, didn't you come to me
with that letter instead of rushing off to the city? It was
a foolish thing to do. You could have been killed."

"I was not," she said perversely. "And would it have
mattered so very much if I had been?"

"That is a ridiculous thing to say," he answered
roughly. "Of course it would have mattered."

"Oh yes. Because of the scandal. The precious family
name!"

"Family name be damned!" he swore. "It would have
mattered to me if even a hair of your head had been
damaged, my love."

Sarah was dumbfounded. "It would?" she managed
to murmur.

"Yes, it would," he repeated. "I think you seem to
imagine I would be pleased to be rid of you, but I don't
know for what reason."

"To put another in my place, of course," she said
sharply.

"Oh! So that's it. Miss Masterson. I suppose some

people talked about her in connection with me and you have been thinking I still cared for her."

"Don't you?"

"I never did," he said with supreme indifference. "Oh, I courted her because it pleased me to foil that silly fop Marchmont, who wanted to win her hand and had no chance with my opposition, that's all."

"All," she said with some heat. "Yet you danced with her at Lady Chesterfield's ball even before me. And I saw you together at Ranelagh," she added, in order to sound less petty.

"The first ball we attended together was a mistake, I admit," he said in a humble tone. "I was piqued by your lack of interest in me and thought maybe I could spark some feelings of jealousy, hence the dance."

"You succeeded," she murmured.

"Did I? I was afraid I had not, but I did not repeat the experiment, for I had no wish to hurt you the more I got to know you. I decided that was no way to win your affection, which I wanted and still do." He turned to look at her, but she was suddenly too shy to meet his eyes.

"What about Ranelagh?" she asked softly. "You were both there, and you were supposed to be engaged elsewhere."

"My engagement was an invention, as you guessed, but I went to Ranelagh to keep an eye on you. I was concerned at the shooting incident and felt someone wished you or your brother harm, and I wanted to know the person behind it. That is why I was there that night, and I think it was the man I had following Dominic who probably saved his life by frightening the attackers before they had killed him."

"We have so much to be grateful to you for," she murmured, twisting her hands together.

"I don't want your gratitude," he snapped. "I will add, too, that I met Miss Masterson quite by chance just before reaching you. I could have cursed my luck that she saw me and put herself in my way. I hoped you had not noticed her, but it seems you had. Is this why you have constantly avoided any contact with me alone and kept me at arm's length?" he demanded.

"I thought you still cared for her and wished you had married her," Sarah admitted.

"You silly little fool. I must say that I had no wish to marry you or anyone else when I made that bet, but after I bumped into you and you grew so cross with me, how could I look at another woman? You have had my heart ever since then." He looped the reins in one hand and put the other around her waist.

The warmth of his body was comforting and exciting. Sarah snuggled up close to him and sighed happily.

"Do you think you can ever learn to love me in return?" he asked, again in that humble tone. "I know I am arrogant and haughty, proud, and many other epithets which you have hurled at me, but can you forget all that?"

"I cannot forget them, because they are part of you and I love you as you are," Sarah told him wonderingly.

The horses slowed their pace and finally stopped, as they no longer felt a hand on the reins. The marquess was too busy showing his wife just how much he cared for her, and she was too busy returning his embraces.

The sound of carriage wheels in the distance roused them both, and the marquess reluctantly picked up the reins once more. "I think it is time we went on our belated honeymoon," he remarked as the horses started forward once more.